"I Told You I Was Leaving, And I Meant It."

"But why?" He shot up from the couch and grabbed her forearms.

"Sonny, this isn't right. I mean, the timing isn't right." Her dark eyes opened wide. "I thought you Southerners did things slowly."

"It depends on what we're doing." He loosened his grip but didn't let go. "Roxie, please stay. You want to. I know you do." He placed a light kiss on her lips. "You do want to stay, don't you? Be honest."

She stepped back, removing herself from his touch. "There are times when honesty isn't the best policy, and this is definitely one of those times."

Dear Reader,

Welcome to Silhouette! Our goal is to give you hours of unbeatable reading pleasure, and we hope you'll enjoy each month's six new Silhouette Desires. These sensual, provocative love stories are both believable and compelling—sometimes they're poignant, sometimes humorous, but always enjoyable.

Indulge yourself. Experience all the passion and excitement of falling in love along with our heroine as she meets the irresistible man of her dreams and together they overcome all obstacles in the path to a happy ending.

If this is your first Desire, I hope it'll be the first of many. If you're already a Silhouette Desire reader, thanks for your support! Look for some of your favorite authors in the coming months: Stephanie James, Diana Palmer, Dixie Browning, Ann Major and Doreen Owens Malek, to name just a few.

Happy reading!

Isabel Swift
Senior Editor

SDRL-7/85

ELAINE CAMP
Hook, Line and Sinker

Silhouette Desire

Published by Silhouette Books·New York

America's Publisher of Contemporary Romance

SILHOUETTE BOOKS
300 E. 42nd St., New York, N.Y. 10017

Copyright © 1985 by Deborah E. Camp

Distributed by Pocket Books

ISBN: 0-373-05251-0

First Silhouette Books printing December 1985

10 9 8 7 6 5 4 3 2 1

America's Publisher of Contemporary Romance

Printed in the U.S.A.

Books by Elaine Camp

Silhouette Romance

To Have, and Hold #99
Devil's Bargain #173
This Tender Truce #270

Silhouette Desire

Love Letters #207
Hook, Line and Sinker #251

Silhouette Special Edition

For Love or Money #113
In a Pirate's Arms #159
Just Another Pretty Face #263

ELAINE CAMP

dreamed of becoming a writer for many years. Once she tried it she quickly became successful, perhaps due to her reporter's eye, which gives her a special advantage in observing human relationships.

To my Reelfoot Lake research team:
Aunt Martha; Uncle Fayne; Aunt Anita;
Uncle George; Bobby; Maurice;
and, of course, my parents.

One

Sorry about your luggage, ma'am," the cabbie said, taking the folded dollar bills from her. "I'm sure it will turn up before the night is over."

"Believe me, it's par for the course." Roxana Bendix sighed and scrambled from the taxi. "This hasn't been one of my better days."

The cabbie gave her a sympathetic smile before he faced front and steered the Yellow Cab from the curb. Roxana watched it merge into the light traffic; then she turned and hurried into the hotel.

The lobby was quiet and tastefully decorated. Roxana walked up to the registration desk and crossed her fingers. If she'd missed him, she would hold the airlines personally responsible. If her luggage hadn't been lost, then she wouldn't have had to waste valuable time arguing with the airline officials about where her baggage was and when it would arrive. The young man behind the desk arched thin brows at her.

"Yes, ma'am?"

"I have a reservation for Roxana Bendix."

"Just one moment." He punched some keys on a computer terminal and squinted at the green screen. "Your reservation was held until five o'clock, Miss Bendix."

"Yes, I know, but I missed my flight and—"

"It's eight-thirty now," he calmly interrupted her.

"I know, but—"

"Your reservation has expired." He smiled as if he had delivered good news. "However, we have other rooms available."

"Will wonders never cease?" Roxana asked with a twist of sarcasm. She was in no mood to offer undying gratitude for small favors. "Could I have a room, please?"

"Of course." He pushed a pen and registration form toward her. "Fill this out, please."

"My luggage has been lost, but I'm expecting it this evening."

"Where did you lose it?" he asked, placing her room key on the desk.

Roxana flashed him a cutting glare. "Somewhere in the friendly skies. Could you ring Sonny Austin's room for me?"

"Sonny Austin..." He checked the computer screen again. "Yes, of course. I don't think he's returned yet, but I'll give it a try."

Roxana finished filling out the form while the young man buzzed the room. She pushed the card toward him.

"I'm sorry, Miss Bendix, but Mr. Austin doesn't answer."

"Good." Roxana released her pent-up breath. At least something had gone right. She picked up the key. "I'm going to wait in the lobby until he returns."

"Very well." The young man shrugged. "We have a coffee shop down that hall," he said, pointing to his right.

"No, thanks." She slipped the key into her purse and crossed the emerald-green carpet to a grouping of chairs that faced the hotel's entrance.

She collapsed into one of the comfortable chairs, then stared at the pair of low heels that were pinching her feet. What a day of foul-ups! Thank heavens she had this time to collect her wits and ease some of the tension from her body.

She brushed wrinkles from her charcoal-gray skirt and blazer, and adjusted the collar of her black silk blouse. She then reached into her purse for her compact and a tube of lipstick. Her brown eyes reflected her weariness as she applied mulberry color to her full lips. She checked her hair, patting the dark curls into place and smoothing the hair at her nape, then put the cosmetics back into her purse. The lobby was empty except for hotel personnel. The young man behind the desk glanced up and gave her a vacant smile.

Roxana felt naked without her luggage, which, she admitted to herself, was stupid. The airline had assured her that it would arrive by midnight, but she would rest easier when it was safely delivered to her room.

Pressing her fingertips to her throbbing temples, Roxana breathed in and out deeply in an effort to uncoil her knotted muscles and ease her tension headache. Her flight from New York to Chicago had taken off an hour later than scheduled because of threatening thunderstorms, and she had missed her connecting flight from Chicago to Tulsa and had had to take a flight three hours later. She'd finally arrived in Tulsa, only to learn that her luggage had been lost and her hotel reservation had expired.

Her stomach growled, reminding her that she hadn't eaten since grabbing a sandwich at O'Hare airport. She had eaten only half of the sandwich, deciding that hunger was better than food poisoning.

Roxana opened her leather-bound notebook and reviewed her notes on the man she was here to meet, hoping that all her delays and frustrations wouldn't jinx this important assignment. A cover story! Her first for *Sportspeople* magazine since joining the staff more than three years ago. It was the chance she had been waiting for, and she was determined not to blow it. Sheila Hawkins had been given the assignment originally, but she hadn't been able to deliver a good, solid article, choosing to focus only on Austin's physical assets and not on his talent with a rod and reel. Bill Tidsdale, the editor, had reluctantly handed the story over to Roxana with a few firm instructions: get Sonny Austin to agree to another interview; focus on his profession as America's number-one angler; and don't let on that you know nothing about fishing.

Bill had shown her a letter from Sonny Austin that chastised the magazine for sending a reporter to interview him who didn't know the first thing about fishing. When Roxana had pointed out that she was in a similar boat, Bill had told her to fake it.

"Our fishing experts are on assignment," he had explained, "so I'm in a pinch. I don't dare send Sheila again, and you're the only other reporter available for the assignment. Austin will be in Tulsa tomorrow for a speaking engagement, and I want you to lasso him there before he sets off for his annual fishing tournament at his Reelfoot Lake resort. If you can wangle an invitation to his tournament, that would be perfect." He had pushed a file folder toward her. "Everything you need is in there. Whatever you do, Roxie, don't let on that you don't know a jig from a jog. Make Austin think that you've been an avid angler for years."

Sheila had echoed that warning when Roxana had talked to her before making a mad dash home to pack for the trip.

"Sonny expects everyone to eat, drink and sleep fishing," Sheila had said. "He was a little miffed when I told him I have never been fishing in my life."

Roxana shook her head at the memory. After reading Sheila's article, she could understand why Bill had decided not to run it. It had read like an article about Mr. Body Beautiful instead of a serious profile on a talented angler. Roxana glanced once again at the sheet of vital statistics she'd been given. They revealed little more than the cold facts: Sonny Austin was thirty-one years old, born in

Memphis and raised in Tiptonville, a town near Reelfoot Lake in Tennessee. She made a mental note that he was a Leo and that his real name was Sonny.

She examined a photo of him and could see what had turned Sheila's head. Sonny Austin was a looker, all right. Blond-haired and blue-eyed, he was teaching a handicapped child the fine art of casting, and the child was laughing and having the time of her life. There was a story here, Roxana had to agree. Sonny Austin must be a generous person to sponsor fishing clinics for the handicapped and the elderly.

Roxana closed both the folder and her notebook and tucked them under her arm along with her purse. It was silly to sit here and wait for him, she thought. She could leave a message for him to call her. In the meantime she could go to her room and relax for a while. Maybe even order something to eat.

She checked her watch. She'd give him ten more minutes and then she'd leave him a message and retreat to her room for repairs.

"Do you think they enjoyed my speech?"

Jasper Collins glanced at Sonny and nodded. "They ate it up. Now we can look forward to the tournament."

"Yes, I'm glad the speaking engagements are over." Sonny shifted in the back seat of the limo. He brushed his hands down his creased trousers. "It sure will be good to get out of these business suits and back into my fishing clothes."

"I know what you mean," Jasper said, running a finger inside the stiff collar of his dress shirt. "These ties are murder!"

Sonny pulled a telegram from the inside pocket of his jacket and tapped the envelope against his fingertips. "This was delivered right before my speech. I hope it's not bad news." He opened the envelope and read the brief message: "WE HAVEN'T GIVEN UP STOP WOULD A COVER INTEREST YOU STOP WILL BE IN CONTACT STOP PINUP MAGAZINE."

Sonny moaned and crumpled the sheet of paper.

"What's up?" Jasper asked.

"That damned magazine is still after me to pose in the buff," Sonny growled between clenched teeth.

Jasper chuckled. "Might do wonders for your social life, Sonny."

"My social life is just fine." He tossed the paper into the small trash bag hanging on the car door. "They're relentless at that magazine. One of their reporters followed me all over Texas last week. I thought I'd never shake her. I finally phoned the editor and told her to call off the hounds, but she just laughed it off. Between her and that dizzy redhead from *Sportspeople*, I've about had it with reporters."

"You've got a problem, all right," Jasper drawled in an accent right out of Nashville. "If you weren't so ugly, you'd have it all together."

Sonny grinned at Jasper's tongue-in-cheek joke. "It will be nice to get back home. I'm really looking forward to the tournament. General Tee is going to be there, and he's all fired up to beat me this year."

"Not a chance," Jasper said with a firm shake of his head. "You'll be fishing in your own waters, and nobody can beat you there. General T. Hayton Bainbridge has copied your technique, but he can't beat the genuine article."

"I don't know about that." Sonny's blond brows met in a frown. "I have to admit that he's got an edge on me. He drew Tim Duncan as a fishing partner, and I'm stuck with that Hollywood starlet Jennifer Vernon."

"Yes, but Duncan is a football player. He probably doesn't know the first thing about fishing."

"I'll bet he knows more than Miss Vernon."

Jasper shrugged off the wager. "You're the king at crappie fishing. Don't give it a second thought. You'll win it easy."

"Hope so. I'd hate to lose my own tournament."

The limousine pulled to a stop in front of a hotel, and Sonny unfolded his body from the back seat and walked into the lobby with Jasper at his side. He headed for the registration desk to check for messages. A petite, dark-haired woman was arguing with the clerk.

"As soon as my luggage arrives, please notify me." She was almost shouting. "Would you do that?"

"Yes, ma'am." The clerk looked past her, and she turned to glance briefly at Sonny. Then she did a double take and whirled to face him.

"Excuse me, Mr. Austin," she said in a voice that sounded as if she had a slight cold. "I'm Roxana Bendix and I'm a magazine reporter for—"

"Not again!" Sonny glared down at her from his superior height. "I've already talked to your editor."

"You have?" Her brown eyes widened in surprise.

"Yes, and I don't want any part of your magazine, thank you." He caught the clerk's attention. "Room 212. Any messages?"

"Let's see..." The clerk turned and checked the box. "No, sir."

"Thanks." Sonny brushed past Roxana and headed for the elevators.

"Mr. Austin, we're talking about a cover story, and I wish you'd just give me a few minutes to explain."

"Look here, lady." He punched the elevator button and glared at her. "The answer is no. N-O. You got that?"

"But the publicity will be a real boost to your charity work. We have a circulation of—"

"I doubt that anyone I'm interested in reaching reads your magazine." He stepped into the elevator with Jasper and frowned when Roxana followed.

"You're wrong, Mr. Austin," she continued. "Maybe you aren't entirely familiar with our magazine."

"That's right. I'm not." He squeezed through the doors before they had fully opened, hoping to escape this pesky reporter who broke into a trot to keep up with him.

"If you'd take a moment to look through our magazine, I think you'll see that it is of great interest to a man like yourself."

Sonny paused long enough to cast her a murderous glare. "Now you're getting nasty. There is nothing in your magazine that could ever be of interest to me!"

Her head jerked a little as if his words had rocked her backward, but she recovered in the blink of an eye and charged on.

"Five minutes, Mr. Austin. If I could have just five minutes—"

"Give her five minutes, Sonny," Jasper urged. "Won't do any harm."

"Thank you!" She turned grateful eyes on Jasper. "Mister—"

"Jasper Collins, ma'am."

"Okay, okay." Sonny surrendered as he opened the door of his suite and let Roxana enter first. "Five minutes."

Roxana quickly walked into the spacious suite and turned to face the tall, blond athlete. Well, he wasn't *that* tall, she thought. His broad shoulders and long waist gave the illusion of great height, but he probably didn't stand over six feet, only six or seven inches taller than herself.

"Have a seat." Sonny waved a hand toward one of the cushioned chairs while he dropped onto the sofa. His body language said quite clearly that he didn't want her company. Jasper went to the bar and removed a can of beer from the refrigerator, popped it open, and sat on one of the tall stools.

Roxana settled in the chair and gathered her composure. The man across from her stretched his long arms along the back of the sofa and glared at her without compromise. He was dressed in a blue business suit, pale blue shirt and striped tie, looking more like an attorney than an angler. His deep tan, however, was evidence that he spent a good deal of his time outdoors; his hair was bleached a burnished shade of blond from the sun. He had a square jaw, a wide mouth with a prominent lower lip, and deeply set pastel blue eyes.

Roxana glanced past him to Jasper Collins. What was he to Austin? she wondered. A business associate, or just a friend? Jasper was in his late forties, Roxana decided as the man ran the back of his hand across his mouth before giving her a small smile. Well, at least he was friendly, which was more than she could say for Sonny Austin.

She took a moment to acknowledge Sonny's stubborn expression before attempting to soften it.

"I know that you weren't pleased with the other reporter from our magazine, and I apologize for that."

"She was one pushy female," Sonny agreed. "And I don't like to be pressured."

"I can understand that. She was a little overzealous and—"

"A *little* overzealous?" he repeated, casting a disbelieving glance at Jasper before looking at Roxana again. "She wanted to take Polaroids of me right there on the spot!"

His statement derailed Roxana's train of thought. "Polaroids?" she echoed, wondering what Sheila could possibly have wanted with those.

"That's right. I was at a tournament—I was *working*—and she told me she wanted to interview me, but all she really wanted to do was see me in my birthday suit."

Roxana felt her jaw drop open, but she quickly recovered and clamped her teeth together. He was kidding, wasn't he? Just pulling her leg, trying to shove her off balance and send her sprawling. She remembered Sheila having said something snide about Sonny having a birthmark on his left hip. Roxana had laughed, believing that Sheila was indulging in unfounded bragging. Maybe she shouldn't have laughed.... Roxanna pulled her thoughts back to the present.

"Let's be serious, Mr. Austin."

"Fine." He leaned forward, propping his elbows on his bent knees. "Let's."

Jasper chuckled, and Roxana breathed a sigh of relief.

"Whatever opinion you derived from our other reporter is your business, but I assure you, I'm not interested in seeing you in your birthday suit." She smiled, glancing at Jasper to share the joke.

"Is that right?" Sonny said in a dubious tone. "And just what *are* you interested in?"

"An in-depth article," Roxana said, getting back on track and pursuing her quest to change his mind. "I'm interested in capturing your personality and your love for angling. I think you're a fascinating subject, and I'm particularly interested in your work with the handicapped and elderly. I think our audience will be just as interested."

"Well, I doubt that." He glanced over his shoulder at Jasper and shook his head, obviously questioning her sincerity. "I must admit that I'm surprised you're planning on writing an article. I thought you were just interested in pictures."

Again he managed to throw her. Roxana stared at him for a few moments, trying to see past his outward calm. "Of course we're interested in an article."

"But you do want pictures, too, right?"

"Well, yes."

A smug smile tipped on the corners of his mouth, and he fell back against the couch cushions. "That's what I thought. And just what did you have in mind?"

"A cover photo, for one."

He nodded. "And inside the magazine?"

Why was he so interested in the photos? Roxana wondered. She decided that he must have a colossal ego and that she was dealing with a very narcissistic individual, so she'd better indulge him.

"Inside the magazine we would have a few shots of you fishing. You know, in your boat or on the dock. They'd be professionally done and show you in your best light."

"That does it!" He threw up his hands and propelled himself from the couch with a surge of energy that took Roxana by surprise. "That's what really bugs me about your magazine."

"I don't quite follow your—"

"Those stupid photos." Sonny cut her off with an angry tirade. "I mean, you're going to take pictures of me fishing in a boat as if it's natural. As if I do that sort of thing all the time! It's ridiculous, and I don't intend to let you make me look like a fool."

Roxana stared at him, completely perplexed. "Are you saying that a photo of you fishing is somehow a misrepresentation? I don't understand, Mr. Austin."

"Don't play innocent with me!" He pointed a warning finger at her. "I know what you're up to!"

"Up to?" she echoed, still dazed by his illogic. "All I want is—"

"I know what you want," he interrupted again. "You want exactly what that other reporter wanted."

"Which is?"

A sly smile twisted his lips. "You want to see me with my clothes off."

"I beg your pardon!" Roxana rose to her feet and stared at him. Despite the severity of his accusation, she found herself amused. He really was enamored with himself! Did he actually think that every female wanted to look at his manly endowments? "You have some gall," she noted, laughing lightly. "Let me assure you that I have no interest whatsoever in seeing you naked!"

"You'll forgive me if I call you a liar." He wasn't laughing; on the contrary, there was a mean look in his blue eyes. "Your five minutes are up."

"And another thing," Roxana continued, not caring that her allotted time had expired, "I don't think that our other reporter acted in such a...a tawdry way. I believe that much of this is due to your own twisted imagination. She has her flaws, but she's a good reporter."

"My twisted imagination?" He glared at her and his face flushed a deep, dangerous red. "All I heard from her was how great looking I was and how she'd love to see my merchandise. It was disgusting!"

"Oh, this is ludicrous!" Roxana grabbed her purse and started for the door. "And *you're* disgusting." As she grabbed the knob it hit her that she was about to bid farewell to her cover story, but she refused to give that a second thought. Sonny Austin was impossible and didn't deserve *any* publicity. Once she told Bill about this, he would understand and cancel the Austin article. She flung open the door and stormed right into the bellboy just as he was about to knock.

Recovering his balance, the bellboy looked past Roxana at Sonny. "I'm looking for the reporter from *Sportspeople*. I was told she might be in this room."

"No, you've got the wrong ro—" Sonny began.

"No, he doesn't," Roxana interrupted. "That's me."

The bellboy smiled. "Your luggage is down in the lobby. Should I take it to your room?"

"Yes, thanks." She fished the key from her purse. "Here's the key."

He glanced at it. "Room 218. That's right down this hall."

"Thank you," Roxana said, grateful for the bellboy's timely presence. She didn't want to spend another moment alone with Sonny Austin and his associate. Her sixth sense registered an unnerving silence behind her. Curiosity gripped her, and she turned around to examine the shocked expressions before her. Jasper glanced at Sonny, and Sonny's face turned a bright red. Both men stared at her as if she were a two-headed, green-skinned alien who had just beamed into their hotel room.

"Sportspeople?" Sonny whispered, then cleared his throat. "You mean to tell me that you're not from *Pinup* magazine?"

Two

Pinup?" Roxana repeated as her mind grasped the misunderstanding. A smile crept to her lips. "No, I'm not. I'm on the *Sportspeople* staff. We seem to have been talking at cross-purposes, Mr. Austin."

"Oh, brother! I can't believe this." Sonny covered his face with his hands and turned his back on Roxana, giving himself a chance to recover from his embarrassment. When he faced her again, he held out his hands in a beseeching gesture. "I'm terribly sorry, Miss...what was your name again?"

"Bendix. Roxana Bendix." Roxana grasped one of his hands and shook it. "Your apology is accepted." She laughed, unable to keep the humor of the situation to herself any longer. "Were you expecting a reporter from *Pinup?*"

"In a way," he admitted, glancing at Jasper and chuckling softly as the irony of his predicament registered. "This is so embarrassing. I just assumed...well, I jumped to the wrong conclusion." He motioned to the sofa and chairs. "Please, let's start all over again."

"Very well," Roxana agreed, realizing that she was being given a second chance at her cover story. In fact, the cards were in her favor now. She had him at a definite disadvantage. She faced the bellboy again. "You can go without me."

"Keep your key," he said, handing it back to her. "I'll use the passkey and put your luggage in your room."

"That's great." She pressed a bill into his hand. "Thank you." She gave him a generous smile before he closed the door. She could afford to be generous now, she thought as she settled into one of the chairs Sonny had indicated. She had Sonny Austin over a barrel.

"Would you like a drink, Miss Bendix?" Sonny asked.

"No, I'd better not. I haven't eaten dinner yet."

"You must be hungry. Could I order something for you?"

"No, that's okay."

"Let me explain," he said, sitting on the couch again. "This reporter from *Pinup* has been hounding me. Heather...Heather—" he paused, his brow creased in concentration "—Heather Rhodes! That was her name."

Roxana swallowed hard to keep the words from spilling out. Heather Rhodes? Her old college roommate? She gave a slight shake of her head. No, it couldn't be, she decided. Heather was working for a New York theater magazine, or at least she had been a year ago when Roxana had bumped into her at a Broadway opening.

"Do you know her?" Sonny asked as if he'd read something in her expression.

"Know her? Who?" Roxana felt her eyes widen. "Oh, you mean the reporter from *Pinup*? No, I doubt it."

"Well, anyway, she followed me all over Texas, and I just received a telegram from the editors saying that they haven't given up. When you introduced yourself as a reporter, I jumped to the wrong conclusion."

"And almost broke your neck," Jasper added with a chuckle.

Sonny nodded and winced slightly. "My mistake, Miss Bendix. Now, about your magazine. Sheila Hawkins has already interviewed me."

"Yes, I know, but we'd like another interview. Sheila's article was less than satisfactory."

"I was afraid of that." A scowl covered his face. "She didn't know the first thing about fishing."

"We all can't be as knowledgeable as you, Mr. Austin," Roxana said, trying to sweet-talk him.

"But don't you think your magazine should have sent a reporter who knew her subject?" he persisted.

"Yes, and we want to remedy the situation." Roxana took a deep breath to launch into her sales pitch, but Sonny cut her off.

"Have you any background in fishing?"

Roxana laughed with what she hoped was a show of confidence. "Do I know anything about fishing?"

"That's right. Do you?"

She glanced toward the bar. Damn him! He wasn't going to let her evade this issue. Jasper lifted his dark brows expectantly, and Roxana decided to throw another curve ball. "I've changed my mind. Could I have that drink?"

"Sure." Sonny glanced at Jasper.

"What's your pleasure?" Jasper asked, slipping off his bar stool and moving around to the array of bottles.

"Vodka and tonic, please."

Silence fell around them as Jasper mixed the drink and brought it to her. Roxana sipped it. It was strong, but she needed something to bolster her courage. Lying didn't come naturally to her, and she wanted to avoid it.

"I know you're busy right now, Mr. Austin," Roxana said, hoping to steer him off the subject of her fishing credentials. "But if I could just have a few hours—"

"You didn't answer my question, Miss Bendix." His eyes challenged her, and his square jaw was set at a belligerent angle. "Do you know how to fish, or has your magazine sent me another reporter who doesn't know her subject?"

Roxana took another gulp of the strong drink. "My editor agreed with the point you made about Sheila not knowing her subject, and that's why I'm here." She glanced at the glass in her hand, surprised to see that it was half-empty now.

Sonny stroked his jaw thoughtfully and sized her up through narrowed eyes. "Why do I get the feeling that you're tap-dancing around a simple yes or no?"

She realized that he wouldn't rest until she told him a bold-faced lie! She forced the words past her lips and wondered if they sounded as false to him as they did to her. "I've fished for everything from salmon to swordfish. When I'm not writing, I'm fishing."

His brows shot up in surprise, then lowered in a menacing scowl. "Funny, I've never run into you before," he said slowly as he glanced at Jasper again.

"I've only recently been promoted to the angling beat," she admitted. She caught the narrowing of his eyes. "But I've been fishing since I was just a kid. I was never into tournament fishing. I like to go it alone. You know, for pleasure instead of competition."

"Oh, I see," Sonny said. "Have you ever fished at Reelfoot."

"No." Roxana swallowed some more of her drink. "I've always wanted to try my luck there. I was thinking..." She paused for more liquid courage, but the glass was empty. "Would it be an inconvenience if I came to your tournament and interviewed you during it?"

He frowned and studied his clasped hands for a few moments. "I'll be busy then, Miss Austin. I'm not sure I could afford the time for your interviews."

"I wouldn't pester you during the tournament. I'd just hang around and soak up the color. After the tournament I'd need just a few hours of your time for an interview."

"So you'd write about the tournament, too?"

"Yes. It would be good publicity, and I promise I won't get in your way while the tournament is in progress."

He mulled over the idea a few moments, and Roxana relaxed, sensing that she was close to her goal.

"Ever fish for channel cat, Miss Austin?" Jasper asked out of the blue.

Roxana felt her heart plummet to her shoes as she lifted her gaze to Jasper. "Not recently." She was getting pretty good at this game. She looked at her glass and held it up. "One more before I go?"

"It's your poison," Jasper said, taking the glass from her.

Roxana took his gentle rebuff to heart. She took stock of herself but she didn't feel dizzy. She was fine. Just a little nervous.

"Here you go," Jasper said, handing her the refill.

"You know, you really should eat something," Sonny suggested. "It sounds as if you're coming down with a cold."

"I'm okay," Roxana said. "I always sound like this."

"Oh?" Sonny smiled. "A husky contralto?"

"That's me. People always think I'm on the verge of pneumonia." She put away more of the vodka and tonic. Jasper hadn't made this one as strong, or was she becoming immune to the liquor's kick? she wondered. "What about the interview, Mr. Austin?"

"Sonny," he corrected. "I guess I could swing it. The pretournament festivites begin this Friday night with a reception."

"I'd love to attend!" Roxana breathed a sigh of relief and relaxed in the chair. Her goal was in sight. He was eating out of her hand, she thought.

"Do you like saltwater or freshwater fishing?" Jasper asked, deflating her momentary euphoria.

Roxana resisted the temptation to glare at him while she answered his question. "Freshwater."

"Then you'll love Reelfoot," Jasper said. "Won't she, Sonny?"

"You bet." Sonny loosened his tie, then shrugged out of his jacket. "Ever fish for crappie?"

"Not in years," she said, balancing herself between the truth and outright dishonesty.

"Well, you should get some fishing in while you're at Reelfoot."

"Then it's okay if I show up at the resort on Friday?" Roxana asked, desperate to get the discussion off fishing and on her assignment.

"I guess so." Sonny glanced toward Jasper to catch his quick nod. "Yes, that will be fine, but I won't be able to give you much time. Even though Jasper is the director of the tournament, I still have a lot to do."

"I understand." Roxana looked at Jasper. "So, you're the tournament director?"

"Oh, I'm sorry." Sonny sat up, snapping to attention. "I should have told you about Jasper. He's not only the tournament director, but he's also been a friend of mine ever since I was a tadpole."

"A tadpole," Roxana repeated with a smile. "How interesting, Mr. Collins."

"Hey, let's cut out this formal stuff," Sonny objected. "I'm Sonny and he's Jasper."

Roxana lifted her glass in a salute. "My friends call me Roxie." She finished the drink and looked at the empty glass. Should she or shouldn't she?

"Let me refill that for you before I leave," Jasper said, making the decision for her.

"Leave?" Sonny asked. "Where are you going?"

"To my room. I'm not as young as you, and I need eight full hours of sleep or more." Jasper mixed the drink and brought it to Roxana. "Nice to meet you, Roxie. I'll see you next week."

"Thank you. It was nice to meet you, too." She waited until Jasper had left her alone with Sonny before adding, "I guess I should be going after this drink."

"Why don't you let me order something to eat? I could use a little snack myself."

Roxana shrugged. "I could eat something light."

"Great!" He clapped his hands and reached for the menu by the phone, studied it, then picked up the receiver and punched a number. "This is Sonny Austin in room 212. I'd like a couple of club sandwiches and a side order of nachos..." He paused and listened to the voice on the other end. "Right. No, that's all for now."

"Interesting combination," Roxana mused. "Club sandwiches and nachos. I'd like to see what you'd consider a heavy meal."

"Too much? Do you like nachos?"

"Love them."

"Good. I'll eat the sandwiches and you can have the nachos." He leaned back on the couch, his fingers laced behind his head. "You must have thought I was nuts earlier with all that talk about seeing me...well, you know.''

"In your birthday suit?" Roxana asked with a teasing smile that made him blush. He was really a very attractive man, she thought as she sipped her drink. Sheila had said that Sonny was shy, and Roxana could see that characteristic in him. He blushed easily for a man, and Roxana decided that she liked to make him blush. "Sheila was impressed with you, but I couldn't imagine her wanting to take beefcake pictures."

She was rewarded again with a slight reddening of his face. He looked away from her for a moment, shaking his head.

"That's what I get for flying off the handle."

"Oh, forget it." Roxana waved a dismissive hand. "No harm done."

His smile was radiant and intoxicating. "Thanks for being such a good sport."

Roxana felt herself smiling back at him and feeling a little dizzy. Was it the kick of the liquor or the potency of his smile that made her heart flutter and her head spin?

"So tell me," he said, unbuttoning his cuffs and rolling up his shirt sleeves, "how long have you worked for *Sportspeople*?"

"Three years, almost four," she answered, gazing at his muscular arms.

"Where are you from?"

"New Jersey, originally, but I live on Long Island now."

"Do you live there with your husband?" He glanced at her left hand.

"No, I live alone." She wiggled her third finger and smiled. "No rings, no strings."

"Where do you usually fish? In the ocean?"

Fishing again, Roxana thought with a sigh. "Forgive me, but I'm supposed to interview you."

"Sorry. I'm naturally curious. You said you've done some swordfishing; how much did the biggest one weigh?"

She retreated to her liquid courage again and finished her drink. White lies weren't any fun, she decided. In fact, she hated them. "Oh, it wasn't very big," she hedged. "Just normal for a swordfish."

"That's one fish I've never hooked. They put up quite a fight, don't they?"

"Yes, quite a fight." She glanced at her watch. "I think I'd better go now and—"

"Go? What about that food I ordered?" he asked, sitting up straight and staring at her with a hint of irritation.

"Oh, I forgot about that." She pulled her lower lip between her teeth in mute frustration. Why had she agreed to dinner? She could have made a swift exit and be in her room now if it weren't for those nachos. This called for quick thinking, she told herself. Quick, before he returned to the subject of swordfish. "Why haven't you ever married?"

He blinked at her, then shook his head. "That question came from left field." Laughing under his breath, he tugged off his tie and flung it across the back of the couch, then freed the first three buttons on his shirt. "I came close once, but it didn't work out." The amusement fled from his face, replaced by a scowl of bitter remembrance.

Roxana roused herself. She'd fallen into a relaxed perusal of the man before her. She liked the
way he'd flung aside his coat and tie, rolled up his
sleeves, and unbuttoned his shirt as if he were in the
company of a friend instead of a stranger. He might
be shy, she thought, but he wasn't uptight. "Were
you engaged?" Roxana asked.

"Yes." He glanced at his own watch and sighed.
"What's taking them so long?"

"It's only been a few minutes," Roxana said
softly. She had struck a nerve, she thought, examining the pained expression on his face. Whatever
had happened between him and his intended still
bothered him. "Was this breakup recent or a long
time ago?"

"Is this for the article?" His blue eyes pinned
her. "Because if it is..."

"It's not," she assured him. "I'm just naturally
curious."

He smiled, realizing he'd been the victim of his
own game. "I'm going to have to keep on my toes
around you. You're a cagey lady."

Roxana shrugged off his comment. "I'm harmless, believe me."

His gaze dropped from her face for a slow ap-
praisal, and Roxana knew that he was seeing her
fully for the first time. A tingle ran up her spine
when she saw the appreciation in his eyes. Chemistry crackled between them, and the room began
to spin before Roxana's eyes.

"No rings, no strings, huh?" he asked in a husky
whisper. "Are the men on Long Island blind or
what?"

Roxana brought the glass to her lips again, only to remember that it was empty.

"Want another one?" Sonny asked.

"No, I've had too many already." She set the glass down, feeling as if there were a tug-of-war going on inside her. Part of her wanted to leave, and part of her wanted to stay and see what developed.

There was a tap at the door, splitting the tension in the room and releasing Roxana from her inner dilemma.

"That must be room service," Sonny said, rising from the couch and crossing to the door.

The waiter entered and set a tray on a table in front of a wall of windows. Sonny signed the check and tipped the waiter, then saw him to the door. Roxana hoisted herself up from the chair and went to the table.

"Let's see what we have here," Sonny said, holding out one of the chairs for her before lifting a silver cover to reveal two sandwiches. "This must be yours." He lifted the other cover and pushed the plate of nachos toward her.

"I can't eat all of these," Roxana said, examining the large portion of chips, cheese and jalapeño peppers. "You'll have some, won't you?"

"I might eat a few." He started for the portable bar. "I'm going to have a beer. What do you want?"

"Water, please. Those vodka and tonics were pretty strong, and I'm beginning to feel their punch."

While Sonny got the drinks, Roxana selected a chip and scooped up a generous amount of cheese.

It tasted delicious, and she realized that she was starving. The peppers were hot, and she felt her eyes tear. Waving her hand in front of her open mouth, Roxana reached for the glass of water.

Sonny laughed and sat opposite her. "Pretty hot, are they?"

She nodded and gulped the water. "Hot but wonderful."

"Your taste buds will adjust after a few," Sonny promised as he picked up one of the sandwiches and took a bite.

She looked at the platter of food and realized that she was having trouble focusing her eyes. Her mind was fuzzy along the edges, and she wanted to kick herself for trying to calm her nerves with vodka. She knew she'd pay for it tomorrow morning.

Roxana pushed the platter toward Sonny. "You can have the rest. I'm stuffed." She sat back in the chair and sighed expansively. "I really should be going." She heard the halfhearted tone in her voice and laughed softly. "Suddenly I'm devoid of energy."

"Did you fly in today?"

"Yes, and my flights were all messed up. I thought I'd never get here." She looked at him through half-closed eyes. "How was your speech?"

"I guess it was okay. They applauded."

"As long as they don't snore, you're a success. Will you be glad to get back home?"

"And how!" He rolled his blue eyes upward, and one side of his mouth rose in a dreamy smile. "Wait until you see Reelfoot. It's beautiful." His hooded eyes found hers. "You might not want to leave."

"I'm sure it's lovely," Roxana said, keeping it noncommittal.

"Who taught you to fish?"

"My dad," she answered quickly. That, at least, was true. She had gone fishing with her father once. Once had been more than enough for both of them.

"So did mine. We went fishing every chance we got. He taught me how to make my first jigs."

Don't let him know you don't know a jig from a jog. Bill's words rang through her mind, and Roxana shook off her lethargy. "What kind of a name is Reelfoot?"

"Indian. Chickasaw, to be exact. Reelfoot was an Indian brave."

"What did he do? Reel in fish with his feet?"

Sonny laughed and crossed his arms on the table, leaning forward until Roxana could see the thickness and length of his sandy lashes and the gleam of his even, white teeth. She sighed wistfully. He was so cute and so easy to talk to, she thought, leaning a fraction of an inch closer to him.

"Reelfoot had a clubfoot, and his walk was different from the other Indians. He walked with a rolling motion, so his people called him Kalopin or Reelfoot."

"How fascinating," Roxana murmured, suddenly feeling very tired again.

"Reelfoot became chief of the tribe and was pressured to take a bride, but none of the Indian maidens made his heart go pitter-patter. So he traveled to Choctaw country and met Chief Copiah and the chief's beautiful daughter, Princess Laughing Eyes."

"Laughing Eyes," Roxana whispered, propping her chin in her palm and trying to keep her own eyes open. Was she just a little bit intoxicated? she wondered. It was a strange feeling, like being wrapped in a cocoon of fuzzy cotton.

"Reelfoot asked the chief for his daughter's hand, but Chief Copiah refused because he didn't want his beautiful daughter to marry a deformed chief from another tribe. Reelfoot decided to kidnap Laughing Eyes, even though the Great Spirit spoke to him and told him that if he did this the earth would rock and the waters would swallow up Reelfoot's village and bury his people."

"Sounds like the Great Spirit meant business," Roxana mumbled.

"He did. Reelfoot kidnapped Laughing Eyes and returned home to the great rejoicing of his people. Laughing Eyes begged Reelfoot to take her back to her own home because she feared the Great Spirit, but Reelfoot refused. They took their marriage vows, and during the wedding celebration, the earth began to tremble and quake."

Roxana roused herself enough to listen to the rest of Sonny's story.

"The Indians tried to run to the hills, but they couldn't run fast enough as the Great Spirit stamped his foot in anger and made the earth collapse around them. The Father of the Waters backed up his course and buried the Indians in a watery grave."

"They died?" Roxana asked. "No living happily ever after?"

Sonny shook his head, and a sadness entered his eyes. "No. Reelfoot and Laughing Eyes died at the bottom of what is now Reelfoot Lake, but their spirits still protect the area. Folks swear that Reelfoot and Laughing Eyes watch over the lake. Experts tell us that we're due for another earthquake, but the locals say that the Indian spirits won't let it happen.''

"Did this earthquake really happen, or is it all just legend?''

"It happened.'' Sonny's gaze held Roxana's in a tender embrace. ''The earthquake reversed the flow of the Mississippi for twenty-four hours. Wait until you see the lake. There are huge cypress trees jutting up everywhere because it used to be a cypress forest before the quake made a lake out of the area.'' He grew silent, and a little smile darted across his lips. ''Are you still with me? You look as if you're about to pass out.''

Roxana snapped to attention, realizing that she was precariously close to falling asleep. ''I must be going. Thanks for the dinner and the invitation to your tournament. I'm really looking forward to it.''

"I hope you can get some fishing in while you're there,'' Sonny said, rising from the chair to see her to the door.

"Well, we'll see.'' She stood up and swayed, but Sonny's hand steadied her. Roxana giggled and pressed a hand to her forehead. ''Too much poison, as Jasper would say. I hope you don't think I do this sort of thing all the time.''

"Of course not.'' Sonny helped her across the room and opened the door. ''I guess I'll see you Friday.''

"Yes, you will.'' She summoned enough strength to stand on her own power. ''Good night.'' Roxana looked up into his face, and her heart skipped a beat.

That chemistry sizzled between them again, and Roxana felt her mouth go dry. She swallowed hard and told herself to leave his room, but her feet seemed to be rooted to the spot. Sonny leaned forward, his gaze glued to her parted lips. Roxana's eyes started to close, only to open fully when Sonny straightened and cleared his throat.

"Good night, Roxana. Sleep well."

Roxana lowered her head and hurried down the corridor to her own room. She told herself that she'd had too much to drink, but she knew that was a measly excuse. She had wanted him to kiss her. She was as bad as Sheila!

Once in her room, she headed for the bathroom and splashed cold water on her face to clear her head. She wetted a washcloth and pressed it to her throat before stumbling toward the bed, where she collapsed. Her temples pounded, and she spread the cool cloth across her face, mentally berating herself for having one vodka and tonic too many. What must Sonny think of her? she wondered. She had wanted to appear professional and mature, and she had gotten sloshed!

But she *had* gotten an invitation to the tournament, she reminded herself, feeling some consolation.

A black veil fluttered down over her mind, and Roxana fell into a deep sleep. Her dreams had no rhyme or reason, focusing on an Indian with blond hair and blue eyes who called her Laughing Eyes and spirited her away to a place where trees were rooted in water.

She awoke with a start and flung the dry wash-cloth from her face. Propping herself on her elbows, she stared at the clock beside her bed. It was eleven-thirty in the morning, and she had a splitting headache. Glancing down at her wrinkled clothes, Roxana sighed and fell back on the bed. She had a one-o'clock flight home, and she wasn't going to make it.

Three

She was late again.

Roxana skipped down the last few steps, sprinted around the corner, and trotted across the lobby to the Copiah Room, where the tournament's reception was under way. As she ran she pinned her name tag to the bodice of her red dress.

Missing flights had become a habit with her lately and one she wished she could break. She'd put in a half-day at work and had thought she could make it to the airport in time for the scheduled takeoff, but she had missed the plane by minutes. She had caught a flight an hour later, which placed her in Memphis two hours behind schedule. There had been a long line at the car-rental booth, but she had finally secured a late-model Mustang, which she had driven at breakneck speed toward Reelfoot Lake, arriving at Point Pleasure four hours late.

The reception had already been in progress, and Roxana had broken all records in checking into her room and dressing for the event.

She glanced at her watch before entering the ballroom. Way to go, she scolded herself. The reception was supposed to end at ten, and it was already nine-thirty. Nothing like being the last guest to arrive.

Pausing in the doorway to catch her breath, Roxana glanced around the room. There were more people than she had expected, she noted as she scanned the area in search of Sonny or Jasper.

A short, white-haired man approached her and squinted at her name tag. His bushy brows shot up, and he stared at her in open curiosity.

"So you're Roxana Bendix," he declared.

Roxana glanced at her name tag. "Yes. That's me."

The man stuck out one hand. "General T. Hayton Bainbridge."

"Hello," Roxana said, shaking his hand. "It's nice to meet you."

"Likewise. Just call me General Tee. Everybody does." He clasped his hands behind his back and examined her through narrowed eyes. "Are you ready to be beaten?"

"Beaten?" Roxana stepped away from him, shaking her head. "No, I'm not."

"Well, get ready." General Tee chuckled, and his brown eyes danced with malicious intent. "I'm going to whip you, good and proper!"

Roxana glanced around in confusion. Was this the right place? she wondered. Or had she mistakenly stumbled into a convention of sadists?

"There you are, Tim," the general said, turning to a tall, well-built man in his thirties. "This is Roxana Bendix."

"Is that right?" Tim held out his hand and gave Roxana a friendly smile. "Well, this is a pleasure. I've been wanting to meet you."

"You have?" Roxana shook his hand and relaxed a little, but she kept an eye on the weird general. "I didn't catch your name."

"Tim Duncan."

"The football player?"

"One and the same." He winked one hazel eye. "Your reputation preceeds you."

"I wasn't aware that I had a reputation." What was he talking about? Roxana wondered. Had he read some of her articles in *Sportspeople*?

"I was just telling her to be prepared," the general said, poking an elbow into Tim's side. "I told her we were going to whip her."

Roxana eyed the general with growing trepidation. Which asylum had he escaped from?

"Sonny has told us all about you," Tim said. "I guess you know how lucky you are."

"Well, no, I—"

"Yes," the general interrupted. "Congratulations."

"On what?" Roxana asked, feeling as if she had walked into someone else's nightmare.

"On getting Sonny Austin, of course," the general said. "He's a good man."

Roxana closed her eyes for a moment while her mind wrestled with this information.

"I mean, it's too bad about Jennifer," Tim added, "but you and Sonny will make an unbeatable couple."

"A couple? Me and Sonny?" Roxana shook her head. Was everyone in this room two feet short of a yard?

Tim Duncan waved at someone behind her. "Here comes Sonny."

Thank heavens, Roxana thought as she whirled to greet her host. Sonny spotted her, and his smile bordered on jubilation.

"Roxie!" He closed the distance between them in two long strides and crushed her to his broad chest in a mighty bear hug.

Stunned, Roxana laughed nervously and tried to regain her composure. She had hoped he would be glad to see her, but she hadn't expected him to be overjoyed.

"I'm sorry I'm late, Sonny, but I missed my flight."

"I'm just glad you're here." He draped an arm across her shoulders and turned to the general and Tim again. "Have you met my friends?"

"Yes," Roxana said, eyeing the general. "General Tee has been threatening to beat me." She turned astonished eyes up to Sonny when he laughed. Did he really find humor in the fact that one of his guests was behaving in such a manner?

"You can try, General Tee, but I don't think you'll be successful," Sonny warned.

"We'll see, we'll see." General Tee glanced at his watch. "I'm going to turn in. Tim and I are getting up at dawn for a little practice."

"At what?" Roxana asked, wondering if she really wanted to know.

"At fishing." General Tee looked at her as if she'd lost her senses. "And I'd advise you to do the same, young lady. I might be as old as dirt, but I can hold my own against upstarts."

"Fishing!" Roxana laughed, suddenly realizing that the general thought she was entered in the tournament. "Oh, I don't need to practice."

General Tee lifted his white brows and glanced at Sonny. "She's pretty cocky."

"She's just pulling your leg. We'll probably see you two out there in the morning."

"Okay." General Tee raised a hand. "Good night, all."

"Good night," Tim said, smiling at Roxana. "May the best man—or woman—win."

Roxana turned to Sonny as the other two men walked away. "Why is it that every time I'm with you, I feel as if I'm talking English and everyone else is speaking pig Latin? What were they talking about?" she asked.

"Oh!" Sonny stepped back as if she'd punched him. "You haven't heard the news, have you?"

"I guess not. What news?"

"Jennifer Vernon backed out of the tournament."

Roxana raised a hand to her forehead. She was getting a headache. "Jennifer Vernon backed out of the tournament. Is that supposed to mean something to me?"

Sonny laughed and caressed her shoulders. "I'm sorry. I'm confusing you."

"I've been confused ever since I met you."

"I drew Jennifer Vernon as my fishing partner, but she can't make it because she's filming a television series."

"So?" Roxana asked, wishing he'd get to the point.

"So..." He smiled, and his hands tightened on her shoulders. "You're my new partner!"

"New partner?" Roxana felt the blood leave her face. "As in fishing partner in the tournament?"

"Right! Isn't that great?"

Roxana felt faint and was grateful that Sonny was holding her upright.

"Jasper, look who's finally here," Sonny said, glancing past Roxana's shoulder.

"Hello, Roxana." Jasper seized one of her hands. "I was afraid you weren't going to make it and leave poor, old Sonny here in the lurch."

"If I'd only known..." Roxana swallowed the rest of her sentence. What was she going to do now? She couldn't be his partner!

"I called your editor Bill Tidsdale and—" Sonny began.

"You called Bill?" Roxana interrupted. "When?"

"A few hours ago. You weren't here yet, and I wanted to ask him if he thought you'd agree to entering the tournament as my partner."

"And what did he say?" Roxana asked, knowing that Bill had given permission but wondering just how far he'd committed her.

"He said you'd love it." Sonny gave her a scolding look. "You've been holding out on me."

"I have?" She felt winded, as if she were running with all her might to keep a step ahead of

Sonny, but he was stepping on her heels and she was afraid of falling flat on her face.

"Yes, you have." Sonny motioned to one of the circulating waiters. "Want a drink, Roxie?"

"No." She held up her hands as if warding off temptation. "I'm not going to make a fool of myself this time."

Sonny's lips flexed in a chastising frown. "You didn't make a fool of yourself."

"I was sauced and you know it." She shook her head when the waiter inched the tray of drinks closer. "No, thanks. I've got to keep my wits about me." She returned her attention to Sonny's previous remarks. "What else did Bill say?"

"He told me that I would be in good hands. He said that when it comes to reeling in the big ones, you're amazing."

"He said that?" She'd kill Bill Tidsdale! Why was he digging her grave? she wondered. Did Bill think she had a glimmer of a chance of pulling off this charade?

"So, you'll be able to kill two birds with one stone."

At the mention of murder Roxana stiffened, afraid that Sonny had read her mind. "What do you mean?"

"You can help me win this tournament and get your interview at the same time. We'll be seeing a lot of each other now that we're partners."

"Oh." She realized that her reaction was less than enthusiastic and forced a smile to her lips. "That's great." She *had* to wriggle out of this, she told herself. Maybe Bill thought she could pull this off, but Roxana knew she would end up with egg on her face. "I'd love to help you out, Sonny, but I can't," she said, unable to meet his gaze.

His blond brows lowered over piercing blue eyes. "Why not?"

"Because...because I didn't bring any equipment!" She congratulated herself for her quick thinking.

"Oh, that's nothing," Sonny said, dismissing her objection with a wave of his hand. "You can rent whatever you need at our sports shop."

"No, no, you don't understand." Panic poured through her. "I...I must have my...my lucky rod and reel!"

Sonny looked at her as if she'd lost her senses, and Roxana couldn't blame him. Lucky rod and reel! Couldn't she have come up with something better than that? She shrugged her shoulders in a helpless way.

"I'm superstitious," she explained. "I've used that same rod and reel since I was a kid. I just can't fish without it."

"Oh, come on, Roxie!" Jasper draped an arm around her shoulders and gave her a squeeze. "Be a good sport. Sonny needs you, so can't you put aside your superstitions just this once?"

"Please, Roxana?" Sonny pleaded.

Looking into his clear blue eyes, Roxana found it impossible to deny him anything. She nodded, feeling as if she had just sealed the lid on her own coffin.

"Great!" Sonny dipped his head, and his lips brushed across her forehead. "I knew you wouldn't let me down."

"A word of warning," Roxana said, hoping to lessen his burgeoning confidence in her. "I haven't been pleased with my fishing recently. I've been having a run of bad luck. I hope it doesn't rub off on you."

"Don't worry," Sonny said. "I think your luck is going to change while you're here."

"How do you like Point Pleasure?" Jasper asked, letting go of her.

"I haven't gotten a chance to look it over yet," she replied.

"I can remedy that," Sonny said, offering her his arm. "Let me give you the deluxe tour."

Roxana slipped her hand in the crook of his arm, eager to leave the party, which was breaking up. "See you later, Jasper."

Jasper waved them off. "Have a good time, you two."

A good time? Roxana glanced up into Sonny's face and felt a painful stab of remorse. It was terrible to lie to him like this, she thought. Why hadn't Bill rescued her instead of throwing her to the lions? She had looked forward to seeing Sonny again, but not like this. Not wrapped in a web of deceit.

He led her outside and stopped before a low brick wall. "Take a deep breath, Roxana. I bet you don't have air like this on Long Island."

Roxana obeyed and filled her lungs with the pure night air. A breeze flew in off the lake and combed through her hair. It would be heavenly, she thought, if she weren't trapped in her own self-created hell.

"Is something wrong?" Sonny asked, bending slightly to gaze into her eyes. "You look...well, unhappy."

"Do I?" Roxana tried to laugh. "I'm just exhausted. It's been a hectic day. Could you give me the deluxe tour some other time? I'm dead on my feet."

"Sure. I'll give you a rain check. You should get a good night's sleep so we can get going bright and early tomorrow."

"Where are we going?" she asked, turning toward him.

"Fishing."

"But the tournament doesn't begin until next week!"

"Right, but we need to spend this week getting used to each other and trying our luck. We'll need to set you up with some equipment, so why don't you meet me at the sports shop around five?"

"Five," she repeated. "Okay."

"We'll get your equipment and be on the lake by dawn."

"Dawn!" Her voice cracked on the word. "You mean you want me to meet you at five *in the morning*?"

"That's right," he said with a chuckle. "You didn't think I meant five in the afternoon, did you?" He shook his head and wagged a finger at her. "You're teasing me."

"Right, right." Roxana glanced at her watch. "But, seriously, I don't think I'll be very alert at dawn. It's almost eleven now, and I've been up since seven."

He stuck his hands in his pockets and rocked back on his heels. "Well, I guess we could skip tomorrow and let you get settled in."

"I'd be eternally grateful," she said before yawning.

"Okay, then I'll leave it up to you to select your equipment tomorrow."

"Great. In that case, I think I'll say good night."

"Roxana..." Sonny reached out and grasped her wrist. "How about dinner tomorrow night at my place, and I'll give you the deluxe tour afterward."

"Sounds wonderful. What time?" she asked.

"Six."

"Which room?"

He laughed and shook his head. "I don't live in the hotel." He turned and pointed to the right. "Just follow this walkway, and it will lead you to an A-frame house near the water. That's where I live."

"Oh, okay. I'll see you at six," she said, gazing into his blue eyes.

His hand slipped from her wrist. "I'll be looking forward to it," he whispered.

Roxana tried to leave at a leisurely pace, but every part of her wanted to break into a run. She felt as if she were living a nightmare as she hurried to her room, closed the door behind her, and released the moan she had kept at bay all evening.

She rummaged through her purse for her address book, then flipped to Bill Tidsdale's home number. He'd gotten her into this, and he was going to get her out of it, she thought as she sat on the bed and dialed. The phone rang six times before Bill's sleep-dazed voice answered.

"Bill? This is Roxana."

"Roxie? What time is it?" Bill mumbled.

"Time to bail me out!" She cautioned herself. Bill was her boss, and she shouldn't press her luck too far. "Bill, I'm at Point Pleasant, and I've just been given the news that I'm part of this tournament."

"Oh, right." He sighed into the phone. "I guess you're pretty sore at me, but what else could I do? Austin called me out of the blue! I didn't know what to say when he asked if it would be okay if you entered the tournament as his partner."

"You could have said no, and you certainly didn't have to sing my praises!" she shouted. "You've got him thinking I'm the best female angler in the country!"

"Just calm down, Roxie. It's not the end of the world," he assured her.

"Why don't I come clean with him before this goes any further?"

"No, don't do that. It's too late for true confessions," he warned her.

"It's never too late for the truth, Bill. It won't take Sonny long to realize that something's fishy—excuse the pun."

"He's not going to watch your every move, Roxie. I've been fishing, and I never pay much attention to the other people with me unless they catch something."

"Which I won't be doing. Don't you think he'll find it a little weird when I don't even get a nibble?" she asked.

"Who says you won't? Fishing is mainly luck, Roxie."

"Bill, I'll be fishing with America's number-one angler! I can't even bait a hook, for heaven's sake," she said.

"Here's what you do. You've got those books I gave you?"

"Yes." She glanced at the stack on the table.

"Read those. They give step-by-step instructions."

Roxana shook her head. "I won't be able to touch a worm or any other kind of live bait," she said with disgust.

"You probably won't use live bait. Sonny will use his own crappie jig."

"That brings up another problem. I'm supposed to equip myself tomorrow. Now, how am I going to do that when I don't know the first thing about rods or reels or jigs?"

"Let the salesman in the sports shop help you. Roxie, you're making mountains out of molehills. Believe me, you can pull this off."

"I think I should just tell him the truth and hope he sees the humor in it."

"He won't," Bill said in a gruff voice. "I've already scheduled this cover, Roxie. You do what you have to do, but don't blow this assignment. I don't want to run Sheila's story. I want to run yours. You got that?"

"Yes." Her sigh was heavy and filled with worry. "I think we're selling Sonny short. He's a smart guy and—"

"You're a smart gal," Bill interrupted. "Get some sleep and keep me posted. I have confidence in you, Roxie. 'Bye now."

Roxie closed her eyes and replaced the receiver. So much for depending on Bill Tidsdale to help her out of this sticky situation, she realized. She was alone. All alone.

She stood up, undressed and went into the bathroom for a quick shower. The sting of the water erased some of her weariness, and she felt more confident as she slipped into a terry-cloth robe and sat on the bed. She turned on the table light and examined the fishing books Bill had given her. By tomorrow she would need to know enough to help select fishing equipment, and by the day after tomorrow she would need to know how to fool Sonny into thinking she knew what she was doing.

Impossible! she told herself. She curled up on the bed and opened the book on crappie fishing, feeling as though she had lost before she had even begun to fight.

Four

—

Staring at the hundreds of rods hanging on the walls and standing in bins in the sports shop, Roxana couldn't discern any differences other than their colors. She plucked a pretty green one with yellow stripes from one of the bins and examined it.

"Find one you like?"

Roxana faced the salesman and smiled. "This one is nice. What do you think?"

"It's one of our cheaper models, made overseas." He pointed to the label. "Of course, it's your decision."

"Which rod does Sonny Austin prefer?" she asked innocently.

"His own, naturally."

Roxana sighed. What she didn't need right now was sarcasm. "Yes, of course, but which brand?"

"His own," the salesman repeated. "The Sonny Austin Ultra-Light." The salesman moved to one of the walls and lifted a black-and-gold rod off its hanger. "I prefer this one, too. It's got a light touch, which is a necessity for crappie fishing."

"I agree," Roxana said, taking the rod from the salesman and trying to appear as if she knew what she was looking at. "Very nice. I'll take it."

"And what kind of reel did you want for that?" he asked.

"Oh, the one that comes with it is fine." She knew she had said the wrong thing when the salesman whirled to face her, his eyes suspicious. Roxana laughed and waved one of her hands in a dismissing gesture. "Just a little joke, Mr.—"

"Palmer. Adam Palmer." He pivoted and went behind a display case. "If I could make a suggestion..."

"Please do!" Roxana stared through the glass at the assortment of reels.

Adam Palmer removed a black one and set it on top of the glass. "This is a popular one in these parts."

"Yes, it's perfect." Desperate to end this shopping expedition, Roxana graced Adam Palmer with her best and most winning smile. "I don't usually do this, but I'm going to place myself in your hands, Adam." She hesitated, letting her lashes sweep down in a moment of propriety. "May I call you Adam?"

The short, fair-haired man straightened his shoulders and cleared his throat. "Of course."

She turned her smile up a notch. "Good. To be honest, Adam, I haven't bought fishing gear in years. I'm equipped to the teeth, if you know what I mean."

His green-eyed gaze roamed from her face to her shoulders and then to her bodice. "Yes, I know what you mean," he repeated, obviously pleased with what he saw.

"But all my equipment is back home. And I can tell that you have expert taste in...many things." She smiled into his eyes, and he wetted his lips with the tip of his tongue. "So I'm going to let you outfit me," she said, crossing her arms, on the glass-topped counter and leaning toward him. "Be my guest."

Seconds ticked by, and Roxana desperately wondered if the salesman was going to fall for her pitch. She felt a twinge of momentary shame, but she dismissed it. If ever there was a time to summon up every ounce of her sex appeal, this was it.

"Well..." She smiled and let her gaze lower to his rather thin lips. "Can I place myself in your hands, Adam?"

He swallowed hard, and beads of sweat broke out on his forehead and upper lip. "You sure can."

"Oh, thank you!" She straightened and glanced around the shop. "I knew I could depend on a Southern gentleman like yourself. Just gather up what you think I'll need. I'm sure you won't disappoint me."

An hour later Adam Palmer had selected jigs, fishing line, weights, a tackle box and a minnow bucket for Roxana. He wrote up a receipt and handed it to her.

"It comes to—"

"Oh, I forgot to tell you," Roxana interrupted, pushing the paper back at him. "Sonny Austin is taking care of all this. I'm just borrowing the equipment."

"Sonny is loaning all this to you?" he asked incredulously.

"That's right. I'm his fishing partner for the tournament."

Adam Palmer looked as if he'd been slapped. "I see. Well, I'll have these things delivered to your room within the hour."

"Thanks. It's room 301. You've been so helpful, Adam. I hope we can see each other again."

He perked up and met her gaze with feverish eyes. "I hope so too. I get off work at five and—"

"Do you?" Roxana hurried toward the door. "Maybe I'll see you around. 'Bye now."

Ducking her head, she headed toward the elevators. How could she have behaved that way? she scolded herself. She had always despised women who batted their lashes and acted like ninnies around men. She never would have believed that she could have stooped to such a level. Of course, ever since she had met Sonny Austin, she had found herself behaving in the strangest ways. Was he bringing out the best or the worst in her? she wondered.

She took the elevator to the third floor and went directly to her room to finish her "homework." The fishing books were scattered across the bed, and she moaned at the sight of them.

Flinging herself onto the bed, she picked up the book she had been reading earlier, and read it aloud. "The standard bait for crappie are small fish, namely minnows. However, on soft summer evenings you can catch them with a fly rod or by carefully laying small popping bugs down among the fish. Artificials, including small spinners and wet flies, will take crappie. So, on occasion, will spoons and small plugs. A combination of fly and spinner is especially good.''

Roxana rolled her eyes and flung the book aside. Hopeless! her mind screamed. How could she learn about fishing when she didn't know a popping bug from a wet fly? She shivered in revulsion. This sounded like messy business and not the sort of thing for a woman who became hysterical when any sort of insect came near her. She held up her hands and throttled the air, imagining that her fingers were clutched around Bill Tidsdale's throat.

Sonny's house was charming, Roxana thought as she approached by way of the winding sidewalk that led from the resort hotel. Point Pleasure's sunset was breathtaking, and Roxana took a few moments to appreciate it before walking up the three steps to Sonny's redwood porch and ringing the bell.

The door opened before the echoing chimes had faded away, and Sonny filled the doorway, looking crisp and clean in jeans and a denim shirt with pearl snaps. Roxana breathed a sigh of relief. She'd worried that she had underdressed when she had put on her jeans, simple white shirt and deck shoes.

"Hi there! Come on in." He stepped back to let her enter the small foyer.

Roxana stepped down into the sunken living room, then looked up at the beamed ceiling and loft bedroom. The furnishings were sparse but inviting, and the hardwood floors were decorated with a variety of colorful throw rugs.

"What do you think?" Sonny asked.

"It's lovely," Roxana said as her gaze moved to a display case over the mantel, which held a simple cane fishing pole. "Is there some sentimental value to that?" she asked, nodding toward it.

"My first piece of fishing equipment," Sonny explained, moving beside her. "My dad helped me make it."

"You made it?"

"Sure did. I caught many a catfish with that pole. I didn't have the heart to throw it away. Did you get your equipment today?" he asked.

"Yes, I selected the Sonny Austin Ultra-Light. I thought I'd give it a try and see if it's as good as it's cracked up to be."

"It is, I can assure you." He tucked his hands into the front pockets of his jeans and heaved a nervous sigh. "Are you ready to eat?"

Roxana glanced sideways at him. Was he nervous about this dinner date? she wondered. Did her mere presence make him shuffle his booted feet and look decidedly uncomfortable? She smiled, stunned by her mysterious power.

"I'm starving."

"Good!" He pulled his hands from his pockets and rubbed them together. "Hope you like juicy sirloin steaks and fluffy baked potatoes."

"I love them."

He motioned toward the dining room. "Right this way. Everything is ready."

He was as good as his word. The table was set for two, and the steaks and potatoes were already on the plates. Roxana sat in one of the chairs and smiled. Her steak was huge, almost filling the plate by itself and leaving barely enough room for the foil-wrapped potato. Roxana took a deep breath, then let it out in a sighing hum.

"It smells delicious." She glanced around the table. "Is there any steak sauce?"

He glared at her as if she'd asked for rat poison. "Steak sauce? What do you need that stuff for? Just wrap your gums around a bite of that steak and you'll be glad you didn't camouflage the taste with that bottled crap."

Roxana resisted the impulse to roll her eyes heavenward. Just what she needed. A bossy man who felt it was his place to change her culinary preferences. Her father had spent the first eighteen years of Roxana's life telling her what to eat, how to eat it and how to enjoy it, and Roxana had vowed she would never allow another person to dictate menus to her.

"You don't have any steak sauce?" she persisted, giving him a generous helping of her stubbornness.

"No." He stared at her, daring her to do something about it.

Roxana shrugged and cut off a bite of steak. "I guess I'll live." She popped the wedge of meat into her mouth, all the while conscious of the man beside her, who was watching her face for every hint of expression. Something ornery prevented her from showing him her true reactions. The steak was delicious, even without sauce, but she would rather have died than admit it to him.

"Not bad," she commented, shrugging her shoulders and wrinkling her nose.

His lips twisted into a frown, and he released her from his scrutiny and began cutting his own steak. The ornery streak in Roxana faded and left her feeling small and petty. What was wrong with her? Why was she exercising such poor manners when she knew better? It was all his fault, she decided. She wasn't herself around him. He created a mass of contradictions within her. He made her want to flaunt her independence in his face while at the same time wishing that she could please him and make him smile. She smothered her potato with butter and sprinkled pepper and salt on it. Glancing up, she was relieved to see that he didn't object.

"You approve of butter on baked potatoes?" she asked with a smile, hoping it would lighten his mood.

One broad shoulder lifted. "Sure," he snapped.

She eyed him warily, detecting a strain of irritation in his tone. "Sonny, are you mad at me?"

His knife and fork clattered to the plate, and he leaned back in a show of exasperation. "No...yes." He shook his head. "I don't know. Just skip it." He glanced at her from beneath lowered brows. "Has anyone ever told you that you're stubborn?"

"Many times." A teasing smile lifted one corner of her mouth. "I don't suppose you've been accused of it, too?"

"I guess I'm a little bullheaded."

She choked back her objection, telling herself not to add salt to the wound. Did he really think he was only a *little* bullheaded? She studied him through the camouflage of her lashes, entranced by the way the muscles in his jawline flexed as he chewed on a morsel of juicy steak. Her furtive gaze moved to the front of his shirt, where the top three buttons had been left unsnapped, and her heartbeat quickened at the sight of the forest of reddish-gold hair on his chest. Roxana swallowed hard and tore her hungry gaze from him. When it came to hairy chests, she was a pushover.

"I have strawberries for dessert," Sonny said, breaking into her wicked thoughts.

"I couldn't swallow another bite," Roxana said, looking at her half-eaten steak. "This is a man-sized steak, and I've done the best I can with it."

He gathered up her plate in a swift, almost angry, motion. "You didn't like my cooking, did you?" he asked.

Her eyes met his, and her heart constricted when she saw the disappointment stamped on his features. "Of course I liked it! I'm just not used to eating as much as you do." Desperate to appease him, she touched his sleeve. "Are they fresh strawberries?"

"Yes," he replied.

"Then I'd love some," she said. "Okay?"

"Well, okay!" He went into the kitchen to get the dessert.

Roxana chuckled under her breath. Who would have thought that Sonny would be so sensitive about his cooking? She greeted him with a dazzling smile when he returned carrying a huge bowl of plump, luscious strawberries.

"And here's the cream and sugar," he said, placing the bowls before her. "In case you want to doctor up the fruit. Personally, I don't think you can improve on nature."

"Are you going to tell me how to eat my strawberries now?" she teased. "I swear, you remind me of my father."

"Your father!" His blue eyes glared with indignation. "Well, that's a fine how-do-you-do!"

"I didn't mean..." Roxana shook her head. "Never mind."

He sat down, regarding her with an expression she couldn't quite decipher. Picking up his fork, he speared one of the strawberries and dipped the tip of it into the sugar bowl. Extending the sweet morsel toward her, he smiled in a way that made her bones melt.

"Did your daddy ever do this?" he asked, holding the fruit to her lips.

"No." The word came out in a strangled gasp.

"Here. Take a bite."

Without hesitating another moment, Roxana slipped her teeth through the sugared berry. She drew back quickly, but was unable to break the power of his gaze.

"I've thought about you a lot since that fiasco in Oklahoma," he whispered.

"You have?" Roxana popped a strawberry into her mouth, desperate for something other than Sonny's enigmatic eyes to occupy her senses.

"Yes. Haven't you thought of me?"

"Of course. I've been looking forward to this assignment," she answered.

"Is that all I am to you? Just an assignment?"

Why was he doing this? she wondered. Was he conscious of this cat-and-mouse game, or was she blowing the whole thing out of proportion?

She glanced around the dining room. "Was this house here when you bought the property?" she asked, trying to change the subject.

"No, I built it."

"A man of many talents!" She busied herself with the strawberries again. "You must be good with your hands." She swallowed the berry with a gulp, hearing the insinuation in her innocent remark. From the corner of her eye she saw Sonny toss her a pleased grin. Chastising herself, she drew on her reserve of strength and pushed herself up from the table. "Will you give me a tour of your house before you give me a tour of Point Pleasure?"

"Sure," he said, rising slowly from the chair. "Right this way," he said, extending one hand in the direction of the kitchen.

Roxana pushed through the swinging door and stepped into the black-and-white-tiled room. Modern conveniences were abundant, and the kitchen counters and floor gleamed with a spotless sheen.

"This door leads to a patio," he continued, opening the door to reveal the redwood deck, where a few chairs and a table were arranged beneath a colorful umbrella. "It's really pleasant out here in the evenings."

"What's that?" she asked, pointing to an adjacent building. "Your garage?"

"Yes, and my laundry room." He closed the door and motioned for her to precede him from the kitchen. "After you."

Roxana submitted to a tour of the dining and living rooms, then climbed up a flight of steps to the loft bedroom. The walls were paneled in knotty pine, and the carpet was a cinnamon bronze that made her think of Sonny's copper-colored skin.

"This is the bathroom," he said, indicating the room off the bedroom, "and that's a balcony." He opened the French doors to show off the roomy balcony, then closed them again. "And this is my bed." His eyes burned with desire.

"No kidding?" Roxana said with light sarcasm, sensing the electricity in the air. She glanced up at the ceiling. "What? No mirrors?" Before he could come up with a clever answer, she turned and descended the stairs again, anxious to leave the intimacy of his bedroom. She felt her control return in the safety of the living room.

"I'm ready for the deluxe tour of Point Pleasure now," she said, turning to face him as he loped down the last few steps. "How long have you owned the resort?"

"The land has been in my family since I was a kid. My folks ran a grocery store and bait shop here, and when they retired, I sought investors and began building the resort." He reached for a gray sweater hanging on a coatrack near the front door. "You'd better wear this. It's kind of chilly this time of year."

"Thanks." She slipped her arms into the roomy sleeves and let him adjust the sweater on her shoulders.

They left the house and followed the winding walkway that snaked through small groves of trees but always provided a view of the lake. Point

Pleasure was located at Champey's Pocket on the northwestern end of Reelfoot Lake. The resort hotel was four stories high, with tennis courts and a swimming pool spread out behind it. In front of the resort was the lake, into which a variety of boat docks and a few piers jutted. A bait and tackle shop sat at the end of one floating pier.

The lake was eerily beautiful, reminding Roxana of the Gothic novels she had read as a teenager. The tops of cypress trees stuck up from the clear water, so thickly in some places that they obliterated the horizon. A bone-chilling breeze blew in off the lake, and Roxana pulled the sweater tighter across her body. Her breath caught in her throat when Sonny's arms wrapped around her waist from behind.

"This lake is big, isn't it?" she asked, hearing the breathy quality of her voice, but unable to do anything about it.

"Yes, very big. It's a detached portion of Fulton County, Kentucky." Sonny's chest lifted and fell against her back, making her feel dizzy. "The area outside the lake is known as the Bend. It's a pocket of land where the Mississippi went awry," he added.

She closed her eyes and tried to think more clearly.

"The Bend is surrounded on three sides by Missouri and on the remaining side by Tennessee. It was a wild and wicked place in the 1800s, populated by men who lived on the wrong side of the law."

She shivered, and his arms tightened. She could feel his lips brush against her hair when he asked, "Are you cold?"

"A little," she answered. Her blood boiled in her veins. Did he feel what she felt? Her heart was beating so loudly, she was sure he could hear it.

"Let's go back to the house." His arms fell from her waist.

Freed from his feverish touch, Roxana set a brisk pace back.

"You should see this place in late summer," Sonny said, draping an arm around her shoulders to make her slow her breakneck pace. "The lake is carpeted with lily pads then."

She didn't trust herself to speak, so she remained silent. Sonny opened the front door, and Roxana hurried inside to break contact with him. She shrugged out of his sweater and handed it to him, then sat down in one of the chairs. He sat opposite her on the couch and stretched his long legs out in front of him.

"I guess I should be going..." she murmured, more than ready to leave him and return to the solitude of her hotel room.

"What's the rush? Sit a spell."

Something in his voice made her protests die in her throat. She curled her legs under her and waited for him to break the sizzling silence. He slid his arms across the back of the couch, and the pearl buttons on his shirt strained for release. Roxana tore her gaze from him and found herself staring at the framed photographs sitting on the mantel.

"Are those pictures of your parents?" she asked, trying to make light conversation.

"Yes," he replied.

"Have you always lived here alone?" She winced as soon as the question had popped out. Why had she asked that? It wasn't any of her business.

"Well, no. I had a... Sarah lived here for a brief time."

"Sarah?" Her eyes found his, and curiosity leapt into her mind. "Is she your old flame?"

"She was my fiancée," he said, looking decidedly uncomfortable.

"I didn't mean to stir up bad memories," Roxana said.

"It's all water under the bridge." He ran a hand across his face as if to erase his thoughts.

"If you don't want to talk about it, I understand." She lowered her lashes and felt him struggle with the prospect of spilling the beans. She had just about decided that he was going to change the subject when he sighed and propped his elbows on bent knees.

"It's funny how you think you know someone when you really don't know anything at all about them," he said. His gaze held hers momentarily, then lowered to his interwoven fingers. "I thought I had found a special woman, but when she moved in here, I discovered that everything about her was a sham."

Roxana folded her arms under her breasts to ward off the pain that was emanating from him. She wished she hadn't opened this particular can of worms, because she hated to watch him wrestle with his bitter past. His brooding frown made her yearn for his smile.

"I can't understand people like Sarah," he started. "She told me she was from a wealthy

Southern family and that she had attended private schools all her life. She told me she was an only child and that she would inherit a fortune when her parents passed on. She said she had a degree in art from Brown and that she had chosen art over ballet, even though she had been assured a career with a ballet company."

"Yes, but could she fish?" Roxana asked, trying to lighten his mood.

A tiny smile flitted across his lips. "No, but I taught her. I don't think she ever really cared for angling, though."

"She doesn't sound like the kind of woman you would be interested in," Roxana admitted. "I mean, she sounds upper crust, and you're so down to earth."

"I know." He ran his hands along his thighs and fell back against the couch. "That's the whole point. I didn't give a damn about her roots or her money or her social situation. I fell in love with Sarah, not with her background."

"Where does the sham come in?" Roxana asked, giving in to her curiosity.

His gaze lifted to hers, revealing a brief flash of pain. "The whole thing was a lie."

"A lie?" Roxanna gripped the chair arms.

"Yes. She was from a family of seven kids, and her folks were sharecroppers. Sarah hadn't even finished high school. She had no real interest in art, and she hadn't been within a mile of a pair of toe shoes in her life."

"Then why did she tell you those things? Was she trying to impress you?"

"I'm not sure," Sonny said. "She knew I didn't care if her family was rich or poor. Fabricating stories was her favorite pastime. When I confronted her with the truth, she laughed."

"She thought it was funny?" Roxana asked, unable to grasp such a reaction.

"She was amused and couldn't understand why I was so angry with her. She told me that everybody told little white lies and that she wasn't going to apologize for deceiving me." A mirthless laugh tumbled from him, and he tipped his head back and stared at the vaulted ceiling. "She felt absolutely no remorse, but the whole world seemed to crumble around me. I felt like the original fool."

"Oh, no..." Roxana reached out in a comforting motion before her hand fell back to the chair.

"I broke off the engagement and asked her to move out. It felt as if I were living with a stranger. I haven't seen her since the day she left, but I heard through the grapevine that she had taken up with a doctor in Springfield. Poor guy. I wonder if he believes the passel of lies she's dishing out to him."

"Maybe she learned her lesson and has mended her ways," Roxana said encouragingly.

"I doubt that very seriously." His gaze rested on her. "It's beyond her powers of comprehension to realize that trust and honesty are the building blocks of any relationship. I think those two qualities are the most important bridges between two people, don't you?"

Uncertainty fluttered through her, and Roxana realized that this was one question she couldn't answer without incriminating herself. She looked away from him, blindly staring in the direction of the front door, wishing for an escape hatch. When he shifted on the couch, she knew he was anxiously awaiting her reply.

"Well, don't you think those are important aspects to any relationship?" he asked, pressing her for an answer.

"Sure," she said in a breezy tone. "And a sense of humor is essential, too, don't you think?"

He shrugged. "I guess so. Some things aren't very funny, though."

Roxana uncurled her legs and stood up. "I'd better call it a night and—" She broke off her lame excuse and stared at the square fingers that gripped her wrist. With an economy of movement Sonny yanked her off balance, and she tumbled beside him before she had time to analyze the situation.

"Sometimes I get the feeling that you don't want my company...that you don't like me," he said softly.

"That's not true," she protested, then leaned back a little when she found herself in close proximity to his parted lips. "I thought we were going fishing in the morning."

"We are."

"Then I should turn in early and get my beauty sleep."

His thumb moved along the inside of her wrist. "You could...uh...turn in early here with me," he suggested.

The blatant suggestion took her by surprise, and she laughed in stunned amusement. "You just come right out with the most outrageous things, don't you? There's no beating around the bush with Sonny Austin."

"That didn't come out right. I didn't mean to sound so crass," he said. His blue eyes twinkled with mischief as his fingers pressed more firmly around her waist. "You won't hold it against me, will you?"

"No. In fact, I'm flattered. It's been a while since I've been propositioned."

"It wasn't exactly a proposition," he argued. "It was a suggestion."

"I'll pass this time."

"This time?" he asked.

Roxana looked at the hand that firmly held her in place. "This time."

He moved so quickly that she wouldn't have had time to elude his roving mouth even if she had wanted to—which she didn't. Her eyes closed as his lips covered hers in a warm embrace that reached down to her soul and sparked a fire in her heart. This is a take-charge man, she thought disconcertedly as his free hand held her head in place while his mouth worked its magic. His other hand released her wrist and moved slowly up her arm to her shoulder. It rested there only briefly before pulling her to his chest. She raised her arms and laced her fingers at the back of his neck. His mouth moved across hers, as if he were seeking the perfect fit. When he found it, the tip of his tongue darted across her lips, outlining them with moist strokes.

"Are you sure you won't stay?" he asked in a hoarse whisper.

"Positive," she answered, her voice trembling with doubt.

He smiled against her lips, then parted them with a certainty she lacked. The rhythmic movement of his tongue sent spirals of pleasure through her. She arched into him and felt his hand move to the back of her knee. He lifted her leg and draped it over his own so that she was sitting in his lap, facing him. His lips slid down her throat, then lower, and his tongue slipped across the top of her breasts.

Roxana tipped her head back, keeping her eyes tightly shut as dormant emotions bloomed into life.

Sonny pressed a kiss in the hollow between her breasts, and she shivered in his arms. He was heavy with desire and growing more desperate by the moment. A hot breath of passion blew through him, and he raised his head and sought her mouth again. Her lips trembled against his, then parted and begged him to enter. Her tongue touched his, moved away, then slipped across his lips. Her soft moan filled his head, driving him wild with a need to know every satiny inch of her.

His hands moved between their bodies to free the buttons on her shirt. Her lace-covered breasts filled his hands, and the hard centers pushed into his palms. His fingers found the front clasp, and he started to unhook her bra, but her hands closed over his, preventing him from revealing her straining breasts to his hungry gaze.

"No, please don't," she begged, pushing aside his hands and buttoning her blouse.

"You don't mean that." There was a definite pleading note in his voice.

"I do mean it." Her hands splayed across his chest, and she pushed herself up from his lap.

"You're not leaving!" He stared up at her, feeling betrayed and indignant.

"I told you I was leaving and I meant it," she said, running her hands through her mussed hair, then letting it fall back across her forehead in a tumble of dark curls.

"But why?" He shot up from the couch and grabbed her forearms.

"Sonny, this isn't right. I mean, the timing isn't right." Her dark eyes opened wide. "I thought you Southerners did things slowly."

"It depends on what we're doing." He loosened his grip on her arms but didn't let go. "Roxie, please stay. You want to stay. I know you do." He dipped his head and placed a light kiss on her lips. When he looked into her eyes, he saw her resolve begin to melt. "You do want to stay, don't you? Be honest."

"There are times when honesty isn't the best policy, and this is definitely one of those times." She stepped back, removing herself from his touch. "I'll meet you at the dock at sunrise," she said brightly. "You can see me to the door if you'd like."

"Roxie—"

"Sonny," she interrupted, placing a finger to his lips. "Please don't ask me to defend my inhibitions."

A rueful smile curved his lips. "You really know how to knock the props out from under a fella, don't you?"

She turned and walked to the door, opened it, then looked back at him. Sonny shrugged, giving up his feeble hopes, and went to her.

"Good night," he said. "See you bright and early."

She rose on her tiptoes and kissed his cheek. "Don't sulk," she teased.

"Can I help it if I'm a sore loser?"

"You haven't lost," she admonished gently.

He squared his shoulders and drew on his good humor. "Right! I've only just begun to fight."

"That's the spirit." She stepped onto the porch and into a pool of milky moonlight.

"The South shall rise again," he said.

Her gaze dropped, then jumped back up to his face. She laughed and waved goodbye as crimson colored her cheeks.

"See you tomorrow!" she said over her shoulder, before ducking into the cover of the night.

She was trembling as she made her way along the path toward the hotel. Later, in her room, she wondered where in the world she had found the strength to refuse him, and then, after a restless night of tossing and turning, she wondered why she had denied herself the pleasure of his company.

Five

As Roxana approached Sonny the next morning she was glad she had kept a barrier between them last night. Juggling a couple of sacks, a tackle box and a fishing rod, she loped down the slight incline toward the pier, where Sonny awaited her in his boat.

Sunrise was not her favorite time of day, but even in her sleep-dazed condition, she found herself bewitched by the beauty before her. Amber light spilled over everything, slowly replacing the violet color of night. The lake sparkled as if strewn with gold doubloons, and the grass under her feet was bejeweled with diamond drops of dew. Her sweeping gaze came to rest on the man who had made her mind reel last night. He stood up, his feet braced apart to keep him upright in the wobbling boat. Spears of sunlight created a hazy halo around his blond head. Dressed in faded jeans, a white T-shirt, and a red-and-black-plaid shirt that had been left unbuttoned, he radiated rugged masculinity.

Roxana paused to get a better hold on her tackle box and to gather her composure. She had realized last night how precariously close she was to falling for Sonny Austin hook, line and sinker, and the realization didn't set well with her. She wasn't the kind of woman to catapult into a man's arms...or so she had thought until last night. It was imperative that she keep her distance from him, she told herself. If she had any hope of continuing this charade, she had to keep her mind on her mission and not on Sonny's sex appeal.

Sonny crossed his arms against his chest and waited impatiently for Roxana to make her way down the sloping ground. What was all the stuff she was carrying? And what did she have on? He squinted against the hazy morning light and shook his head in amusement. She was really decked out—khaki pants, a yellow sweater and a khaki fishing vest. Her floppy-brimmed khaki hat shadowed her face and let her ebony curls escape in shiny profusion. Sonny's smile grew.

"Good morning!" he called, waving one hand in a sweeping greeting. "Need any help with your gear?"

"Not yet!" she called back, then scrambled down the rest of the way and gingerly tiptoed along the pier toward him. "Have you been waiting long?"

"Only a few minutes. Here, let me take some of that stuff." He reached out and grabbed a couple of sacks and her tackle box. "What have you got in these sacks?" he asked, feeling their heavy weight.

"Some things I picked up in the sports shop. Line and a reel and—"

"A reel?" He glanced at the rod she held. "You haven't outfitted that rod yet?"

"No. I—I...it's new."

"I know that," he said a bit testily, "but I thought you'd be all ready to get going."

"What's the hurry? We have all day." She eyed the bobbing boat and wondered how to get in without breaking her neck. "How about lending me a steady hand while I hop in?"

"Sure." He set her things down in the center of the boat and held out one large hand. "Grab on."

Her hands slipped into his, and she held on for dear life as she stepped into the boat. Quite suddenly, the bass boat tipped to one side, throwing her off balance and into Sonny's arms.

"Whoa, there, sugar britches!" he said, laughing as his arms tightened around her waist to steady her.

Her heart leapt to her throat and settled there. Roxana closed her eyes and glimpsed heaven. Sugar britches? She smiled, thinking that she would consider that a chauvinistic remark from any other man, but coming from Sonny, it was precious. Opening her eyes, she drew back from him and cautioned her runaway heart.

"Sugar britches?" she asked, her tone light and teasing. "Is that a compliment or what?"

"What do you think?" he teased back, his arms still holding her.

"I think it's original," she answered, then removed herself from his all-too-tempting embrace. "Where do you want me to sit?"

"Right here." He gently pushed her down into a chair that was bolted to the front of the boat. "Did you buy that outfit at the sports shop too?"

"Yes. Is there something wrong with it?"

"No." He turned and sat near the motor. "But you're going to get warm in that sweater."

"It's chilly out here," she remarked crossing her arms to keep warm.

"In another couple of hours the sun will heat up the atmosphere." He jerked the starter cord, and the motor sputtered to life, then settled into a powerful hum. "You can outfit your rod while I steer us toward my favorite fishing hole."

"Sonny, I was thinking..."

"What?" he asked, twisting around to face her.

"I'd love to see the lake. Why don't you take me on a tour of it before we start fishing?" She held her breath as he considered the request. Maybe it wasn't a good idea to postpone the inevitable, but she still had a few wrinkles to iron out in her plan—like how to outfit her fishing rod and reel while getting used to the rocking motion of the boat. Last night she had convinced herself that she could hoodwink Sonny into thinking that she was all she was cracked up to be, but she was having her doubts this morning. She glanced around the boat, feeling out of her element and more than a little afraid.

Remember the cover article and how it will propel you up the ladder of success, she reminded herself. *Don't think about the water and the fish. But most of all, don't think of those awful lies you've been handing him. Oh, the tangled webs we weave...*

"The fish are biting now and—"

"Sonny, please?" she begged, leaning forward and placing her hand on his sleeve while her eyes did most of the work for her.

"Well..." He met her pleading gaze and felt his insides melt. "Okay, why not?"

"Great!" she cried. Her hand slipped off his sleeve as she sat back in satisfaction.

"We'd better put our life jackets on before we get under way." He pulled two lightweight vests from a storage bin near the motor and handed one to her.

"Good idea," Roxana said, taking it from him and examining the belts and fasteners. She pushed her arms through the holes and fumbled with the front closures.

"Here, let me help you," Sonny said, pushing aside her fluttering hands and hooking the belts into the loops with practiced ease. "There you go."

She averted her face from him, feeling her skin flush with the memory of a few hours ago, when he had been intent on undressing her instead of dressing her.

The boat sped from the pier and sliced through the golden-hued water. A stiff breeze cooled her skin, and Roxana lifted her face to it, letting the chilly air eradicate her nervous tension. Shouting above the roaring motor, Sonny pointed out pockets of land and water called Blue Basin, Green Island Point and Swan Basin. He steered the powerful outboard through Samburg Ditch, and Roxana's gaze whipped this way and that to catch all the points of interest. Giant cypress trees created a cathedral ceiling in places, and along the shore their gnarled and twisted trunks rose in majestic splendor. They lined the banks like rows of sentries, guarding the lake from unseen danger. As the boat drew nearer to the banks Roxana strained forward to inspect a rippling on the water's surface.

"What's that?" she shouted, pointing to the disturbed water. Her eyes played tricks on her, and she thought she saw a small branch move along the smooth surface.

"Water moccasins," Sonny shouted back.

"Oh." She lowered her arm, then suddenly realized what he had said. Jerking backward, she felt her eyes widen in terror. "You mean...those are snakes!"

"Yes, this place is full of them. They're poisonous," he said as calmly as if he were talking about something as innocuous as a newborn kitten. Searching the water near the boat, Roxana felt her terror develop into near hysteria. Now she knew what dangers the cypress sentries were guarding against! she told herself.

Sonny tore his gaze from the writhing snakes a few yards from the boat and faced Roxana again. Now what? he wondered, knitting his brows in confusion as he examined her saucer-size eyes and ghostly pallor.

"What's wrong with you? Are you sick?" he asked with concern.

"Snakes!" The word exploded from her pale lips. "Let's get out of here before they attack us!"

"They aren't going to attack us," he said with a chuckle. "For heaven's sake, get hold of yourself.

Haven't you ever been around cottonmouths before?"

"Cottonmouths?" she repeated, her eyes wild and terror-filled. "Are they here, too?"

"They're one and the same," he said. "Water moccasins are called cottonmouths because when they open their mouths, it's all white inside." He rested a hand on her knee. "Settle down, Roxie. You're safe."

Roxana stamped down her fear with some difficulty. If Sonny hadn't been so calm and dependable, she knew she would have come completely unglued. But he was right, she thought. As long as he was with her, she was safe. She swallowed a wedge of fear in her throat.

"Are you sure they won't bother us?" she asked, giving the spot another wary glance.

"Not unless we make them mad by teasing them or something—which we won't." He winked one blue eye and slid his hand off her knee. "Nothing to worry about, Roxie," he assured her, sensing her fear. "Those old cottonmouths don't want any trouble. When I was a kid, I used to hunt them."

"Why?" Roxana asked, unable to understand such a peculiar death wish.

"You know how kids are," he said with a shrug. "One time I aggravated one and he took after me." He laughed at the memory. "I had this old single-shot gun that I'd use to shoot at them. I guess I missed that snake five or six times before I finally picked up a fallen branch and beat him off."

"The snake was chasing you?" Roxana asked, trembling at the thought.

"Yes, they'll do that if you get them mad enough. They rear up and hiss at you, and do they stink!" He wrinkled his nose in distaste. "Talk about bad breath. Whew!"

"You've been close enough to smell their breath?" she asked incredulously. She wrapped her arms around herself and drew up into a tiny bundle of quivering nerves.

"Sure." He glanced across the lake and chuckled. "I had a few years scared out of me once. I was fishing—minding my own business—when this big old water moccasin fell out of a tree right into my boat. I jumped out of the boat and so did he." He paused and laughed. "Lordy! I scrambled back into that boat so fast, I still don't rightly recall how I did it. All I know is that in a split second I was revving up the motor to get the hell out of there! It was so fun—" He broke off his narrative when Roxana's fingers bit painfully into his forearm. "What is it?"

Her gaze was glued to a spot over his head, and Sonny looked up at the tree branches spreading across the sky. It took him a few moments to follow her train of thought.

"I'm sorry. Here I'm telling you all these horror stories when I meant to make you feel better," he said.

"Let's...get...out...of...here!" Her voice rose with each word, ending on a shriek.

He started to give her a stern lecture on self-control, but he could see that she was beyond any level of logical thought. As Sonny steered the boat toward Buzzard Slough, Roxana slowly relaxed.

"I guess it's time to try our luck, don't you?" Sonny asked.

"What about the rest of the tour?"

"There's not much else to see. Besides, in another few hours the fish will stop biting. I'll continue the tour after we catch a few."

Roxana sighed heavily. So much for wasting time, she thought. Sonny was determined to force her hand. She glanced at the rod lying beside her. How was she going to handle this? Alarm coursed through her when the motor died and the boat floated a few yards from shore.

"This is a good spot," Sonny announced enthusiastically. "Can't wait to wet my line."

"My hands are still shaking," Roxana said, holding them up and making them shake more than was necessary. "Could you put my rod and reel together for me while I settle my nerves? I'm still a little upset over those snakes."

"Why, sure. Let me have it," he replied, grasping the rod and reaching for the two sacks that held the reel and line.

Roxana smiled and congratulated herself. That wasn't so hard, she thought with elation. Maybe this wasn't going to be as impossible as she had thought. She watched carefully as Sonny fitted the reel on the fishing rod, then threaded the line through it. It was similar to threading her sewing machine, and she realized she could probably do it herself next time.

"What kind of bait are you going to use?" he asked, popping open the tackle box that held the jigs Adam Palmer had selected for her.

"Uh..." She stared at the shiny objects, then pointed to a pretty one. "How about this?" Doom engulfed her when Sonny's gaze impaled her.

"Are you sure you want to use a popping bug?" he asked in disbelief.

Roxana cleared her throat nervously and pretended to reconsider her choice.

"Well, no, I guess not." She gave a little shrug. "You know these waters better than me. What would you suggest?"

He scrutinized the collection of lures, then selected one. "Why don't you try this little crappie jig?"

"Why not?" Jubilation replaced the doom, and confidence poured back into her. "A crappie jig should catch crappie."

He made a comical face at her. "You Easterners!"

"What do you mean by that?" she asked indignantly.

"The way you talk," he explained. "It's not CRAP-pea. It's CROP-pea. I swear, you Yankees really mess up the English language every chance you get."

Roxana squared her shoulders and narrowed her eyes to smoldering slits. "If anyone is guilty of ruining the language, it's the Southerners!"

"What?" He gave her an incredulous glare. "Who are you kidding? Let me ask you this—how do you Yanks get 'i-deer' out of 'i-de-ah'?"

"Well, would you kindly show me the word 'ain't' in the dictionary!" she retorted hotly.

His brows lowered in a menacing scowl. "I've never said 'ain't' in my life!" he exclaimed.

"And I've never pronounced 'idea' with an 'er' at the end of it in my life!"

Several tense seconds ticked by before a corner of Sonny's mouth quirked in amusement. The minuscule movement was enough to break through the heat of the moment, and Roxana realized that they were nose-to-nose, glaring and growling at each other like two bulldogs with a bone between them. She dissolved into giggles as Sonny's smile overtook him and laughter brought tears to his eyes.

"What's wrong with us?" Roxana asked between giggles. "What a thing to fight over!"

Sonny wiped his eyes, and his laughter subsided. "How we say things isn't nearly as important as what we say to each other."

The truth of that statement had a sobering effect on her. Roxana shifted uncomfortably, feeling a niggling of shame. Yes, how true, she thought. And what have I said to him? Nothing but lies. Just like Sarah.

"Hey, you're not mad at me, are you?" he asked.

She turned startled eyes on him. "Mad? No, of course not." She took the rod and reel from him, anxious to busy herself with something other than her own guilt. "Let's fish," she said, surprising even herself. Who would have thought that she would ever voice that command?

"Right!" Sonny grabbed his rod and reel, checked the lure at the end of the line, then deftly cast it out. The line sang sweetly, then was silenced by a tiny plop as the lure hit the water a few feet from the bank. "I bet there's a whole mess of crappie hiding in that shade by the bank."

Roxana nodded absently, seized by her own incompetence. Sonny had cast out his line in a fluid motion that she had no hope of copying. She stared at her rod and reel and wondered how it worked. Fingering the trigger, she pressed it in and the line fed out, the lure plunking against the floor of the boat. She cranked the line back in slowly, her mind racing for a way out of this situation.

"What are you waiting for?" Sonny asked, staring at the top of her head.

"Nothing." She pressed in the trigger again, trying to get a feel for it.

"You can't catch any fish that way," he declared.

"I know it!" She glared at him. "I'm just getting used to this rod and reel. Do you mind?"

Sonny lifted one shoulder in a casual shrug. "Okay, okay! You don't have to bite my head off." His body stiffened. "Hey! I've hooked one!"

"You have?" She dropped her own equipment and watched him expertly reel in the struggling fish. "What is it?" she asked excitedly.

"A big old bass. Give me the net," he commanded, trying to steady the fish.

"The net?" She glanced around the boat, then grabbed a small net. "Here," she said, pushing it toward him.

"Net it for me, will you?"

Roxana shuddered at the thought, but knew she had to obey. Leaning over the side of the boat, she dipped the net into the water. After several attempts she managed to slip it under the wriggling fish. Her breath escaped in a sigh of relief as she lifted the netted fish from the water.

"He's a big one," Sonny noted, resting his fishing pole against one shoulder as he grabbed the squirming fish.

Roxana watched carefully as he seized the fish's lower lip and wrestled the hook from it with a pair of tiny pliers. Her mouth dropped open in dismay when Sonny pitched the fish over the side of the boat, then pocketed the pliers.

"What did you do that for?" she asked in confusion.

"I'm fishing for crappie, not bass," he replied.

She nodded, not really understanding why he would throw such a big fish overboard. Wasn't that the whole point of fishing? she wondered. To catch them *and* keep them?

"Let me try that out." Sonny retrieved her rod and reel and, with a simple flick of his wrist, cast out the line.

If he had captured a rainbow for her, it wouldn't have pleased her more. When he started to reel in the line, she grabbed his shirt sleeve.

"No! Leave it out there!" she cried with desperation.

"Okay. Here you go," Sonny said, placing the rod in her hands, then gathering up his own. He cast out, and his lure dropped a few feet from hers. Smiling, he sat in the chair nearest the motor.

The boat rocked slightly beneath her feet, and Roxana looked over her shoulder at the empty chair behind her. Just as she was about to sit down, the pole quivered in her hands.

"You've got one!" Sonny's voice rang out, adding to her panic.

The pole vibrated again, and Roxana stopped thinking rationally and reacted on pure adrenaline. Forgetting the crank on the reel, she jerked the rod backward with all her might. The boat rocked violently, throwing her completely off balance. The line whiped over her head, and in a flustered moment of comprehension, she knew she was doomed. In the next instant she felt herself plunging backward, and then the cold lake claimed her. Her survival instincts took over, and Roxana flailed helplessly, opening her mouth for air and choking on water.

"Help! Sonny! Help me!" Her voice was ragged and high-pitched, bordering on a scream.

It took a few moments for Sonny to realize that the blur that had whipped past him had been Roxana. Her bloodcurdling scream galvanized him, and he stood up, taking stock of the situation. Roxana was a few feet from the boat, treading water. A burst of laughter escaped him.

"What are you doing in there, sugar britches?" he asked. "Are you going to catch that fish with your bare hands?"

"I'm drowning! I can't swim! Help me!" she shrieked, flapping her arms wildly.

Sonny shook his head, but his amusement faded swiftly when he saw her new rod and reel floating near her. He quickly tore off his life jacket, plaid shirt and T-shirt, and dived into the water to retrieve the expensive fishing equipment. When he swam past Roxana, she grabbed for him, but he eluded her and caught the fishing pole just as it began to sink.

In her fit of hysteria Roxana glimpsed something long and straight floating near her just as Sonny grabbed for it. Black terror erupted within her, and she knew, without a doubt, that she was close to insanity. Visions from her childhood of old Tarzan movies flitted across her mind: Tarzan battling a monstrous crocodile or a...

"Snake!" she screamed.

Sonny whipped around in the water. "Where?" He saw nothing except Roxana, who was still floundering and screaming a few feet from him. He swam to the boat and threw the rod and reel into it, then swam back to her. He ducked as her arm swung wildly, but he was a second too late. Her elbow smashed into his forehead, and he saw stars.

"Roxie, calm down! You're going to beat me black and blue!" he said, grabbing her arms and pinning them to her sides. "You're not going to drown! You have a life jacket on, damn it!"

"What did you do with that snake? Did you kill it?" she asked in hysterics.

"What snake?" he growled, losing patience with her. "There wasn't any snake. That was your fishing pole."

"My...oh." Her legs stilled when she felt his arms encircle her waist. "Get me out of here."

"With pleasure." He hauled her toward the boat, his legs moving in a strong scissor stroke. Treading water behind her, Sonny waited for Roxana to grab the boat, then planted his hands on her bottom and unceremoniously pushed her over the side. Catching his breath, he then hoisted himself into the craft, landing in a wet heap. His heart thudded dully in his chest. "You can't swim?" he asked between labored breaths.

"No, I never learned how." She gasped, pushing her hair back from her forehead. "My hat!" She looked around, then pointed to the water. "There it is!"

"And there it will stay," he declared firmly.

"You're not going to get it for me?"

"No, I'm not. You're lucky I saved your rod and reel."

Roxana levered herself into the chair and kicked at the rod and reel. "You saved that thing before you saved me!"

"I *knew* it couldn't swim and that it didn't have a life jacket on to keep it afloat," he retorted.

Hearing the growling impatience in his voice, Roxana wrestled her fear under control and examined Sonny's menacing scowl. "I thought...when I saw that fishing pole, I thought it was a water moccasin. I'm sorry. I didn't fall in on purpose!"

An uneasy silence descended while they caught their breath. Roxana felt weak and limp-limbed but safe, now that she was back in the boat. Sonny sat at her feet in a pool of water. His bare chest rose and fell with his heavy breathing, and drops of water sparkled amid the wet hair plastered against his chest. He lifted a hand and pushed back his blond hair.

"You've hit your head on something," Roxana said, leaning forward and touching the red bump above his right eyebrow.

"No kidding?" His voice dripped with sarcasm. "You're responsible for that. You almost poked my eye out with your elbow!"

"I...I did?" Roxana covered her lips with her hands, but couldn't keep from laughing. He glared at her, and for a moment, she thought he was going to strangle her, but then he grinned and chuckled under his breath. "I'm sorry, Sonny. Thanks for coming to my rescue," she said apologetically.

He leaned back, propping himself on stiffened arms, and regarded her with a tenderness that made her heart skip a beat. "How can you enjoy fishing when you're scared of water?"

"I don't know. I just do. There's no rule that you have to know how to swim to be able to fish, is there?" she asked.

"No, but I would think it would be a handicap."

"It hasn't been until today. It's a good thing I had this life jacket on."

Sonny sighed and let his gaze wander along the bank. "This hasn't been a very good fishing trip, but it's been one adventure after another, hasn't it?" he asked, turning his gaze to Roxana.

"Yes, but I think I've had all the adventure I can take for one day," she replied.

"Why did you jerk the rod back like that? Why didn't you just reel in that fish?"

"I...I don't know." Roxana stared at her hands in her lap. The pleasure of the moment faded with the reminder of her deceit. The truth trembled on the tip of her tongue.

"If I didn't know better, I'd say that I intimidate you," Sonny admitted.

"That's it!" She raised her gaze to his in quick agreement. "I mean, you're the best, and I...I don't think I can hold my own against you."

"Oh, that's silly," he admonished. "We're a team. We have to pull together."

"Yes, but I'm still nervous around you. I'm afraid I'll disappoint you." No truer words were ever spoken, Roxana thought with a twinge of guilt. In fact, she was bound to disappoint him. She'd be lucky to leave Reelfoot in one piece if he discovered the string of lies she had fed him. Sonny's hands covered her thighs, and Roxana's heartbeat quickened as he rose to his knees to face her.

"Don't talk like that. You could never disappoint me," he assured her.

"Oh, Sonny..." Emotion lodged in her throat, and she wished she could confess her sins and beg for forgiveness.

"So you fell overboard. That's nothing! I've fallen into this lake more times than I can count," he admitted.

"It's not that..." Her voice died along with her courage to set things right.

"What is it?" he asked in an intimate whisper.

She parted her thighs, and his upper body slipped between them as her hands framed his face. Her index finger touched the swelling bruise above his eyebrow. "I don't want to hurt you," she murmured lovingly, feeling foolish for her hysterics.

His smile was gentle. "Hell, you didn't hurt me. Maybe you knocked some sense into me."

Roxana closed her eyes. He didn't understand. He thought she was talking about physical wounds when she had been talking about much more serious afflictions. She started to explain, but his lips silenced her. His mouth moved warmly over hers, and his hands caressed her waist. Roxana ran her hands over his damp shoulders before burying her fingers in the wet, slick hair that covered his chest. She opened her mouth to receive his roving tongue, and a weakness stole though her.

Heaven help her! How could she keep him at arm's length when she wanted him with every fiber of her being? she wondered. One touch and she was crazy with longing. Every time she gave him an inch, she begged him to take a mile. She couldn't keep herself in check, even though her common sense was screaming at her to end the kiss. Her tongue parried with his. Her hands flattened against his chest. Her lips clung to his in blatant supplication. He was the one who broke away with a little gasp.

"You're soaked to the skin, lady," he said, plucking at the sleeve of her wet sweater.

"I know." Roxana grimaced. "This thing itches! Would you mind turning around for a minute?"

He shrugged and obeyed. Roxana glanced around to make sure they were alone, then removed the life jacket and her vest. She pulled the yellow sweater over her head, dropped the garment to the floor of the boat, then slipped on the vest again and buttoned it up the front.

"All done," she announced. Sonny got to his feet and turned to face her. His gaze took on an appreciative glimmer.

"Nice. Very nice." He cleared this throat and started the motor again. "I'll take you to one of my favorite spots on this lake."

"To fish?" she asked nervously.

"No." He winked at her. "To goof off."

He sat by the motor, pulled on his T-shirt, then steered the boat over the glassy surface of the lake. "I want you to see Jasper's place."

"What part of the lake does he live on?"

"A place called James Camp. It's named after my great-great-grandfather. Everyone called him James because he wouldn't tell anyone his last name. Finally he told people that his name was James Austin, but most folks say that was an alias, since he came from Austin, Texas."

"Why didn't he want to reveal his real name?" she asked curiously.

Sonny flashed her a conspiratorial grin. "I guess he was in some sort of trouble with the law. My guess is that he was a card shark who hadn't been sharp enough."

"How interesting. You know, this place is alive with legends and fascinating stories. Someone should write a book about it."

"I agree." He cut the motor and let the boat float toward a ri   pier. "Why don't you?"

"Me?" She laughed lightly. "I've never..." The rest of her excuse floated away as the idea took seed in her mind. Yes. Why not? She was a writer, and this was a hotbed of intrigue.

"Doesn't look like Jasper is around. He's probably at the lodge, since there's so much to do right now." Sonny held out his hand to help her from the rocking boat, and he kept her hand tightly in his, even when she was on solid ground again. "Wait until you see the graveyard behind Jasper's house," he said. "There's a story etched on every tombstone."

"This is Jasper's house?" Roxana asked.

"Yes, he built it."

"I've never seen a real log cabin before. It's adorable!" she said. The cabin was one story and tiny, with only two rooms to it.

"Have you ever seen one of those before?" Sonny asked, pointing to a small house behind it. "And it's not a chicken coop."

Roxana laughed, noting the crescent moon carved in its door. "An outhouse!" she exclaimed.

"Right, and don't say it's adorable. Indoor plumbing is the best invention since sliced bread."

He then guided her around to the back of the outhouse and led the way along a path that cut through cypress and willow trees. "The graveyard is right back here," he said. "It's been here since the early 1800s."

They entered a clearing where slabs of roughly hewn granite jutted up from the carpet of grass. Somber weeping willows bordered the clearing, their leafy heads bowed in permanent condolence.

"Come on." Sonny was whispering, in reverence to the sacred ground. "I want to show you something."

She followed, picking her way carefully among the few dozen graves. Sonny stopped before one, and Roxana leaned forward to read the inscription.

"Here lies Jake the Snake. Knife-slashed at a dance." Roxana turned astonished eyes on Sonny. "Good grief! They didn't mince words, did they?"

"No. Look at the next one."

"Here lies Greenberry Watson," Roxana read in a whisper. "Assassinated!"

Sonny laughed and pulled her to the next one. "Look at this. Hank Bishop. Pistol-whipped," he read to her.

"Heavens! Did anyone buried here die of natural causes?" she asked, quickly scanning the surrounding headstones.

"A few, but most of these poor souls were victims of a violent era. I told you that this place was a haven for convicts and gunslingers back in the 1800s."

"Yes, but..." She leaned forward to read a tombstone that had a cross on top of it. "Old Maid Annabell Brimley." She glanced up at Sonny and frowned. "What a quaint custom! Calling this poor woman an old maid just because she enjoyed her independence too much to give it up." Sonny shrugged helplessly, and Roxana looked back to the line below the woman's name. "Choked to death by the Quake." She straightened slowly. "What does that mean?"

Sonny ran a finger over the date and year etched in the stone. "December 17, 1811. That was the day after the big earthquake started. My great-great-grandmother kept a diary during that time, and she wrote that the atmosphere was so completely saturated with sulfurous vapors caused by the earthquake that at noon it seemed to be midnight."

"Good heavens! No wonder this poor woman choked to death," Roxana exclaimed.

"The hardest shock came on February 7, 1812," Sonny continued, holding Roxana's hand and stroking her inner wrist with his thumb. "My great-great-grandmother wrote that the waters of the Mississippi gathered up like a mountain, rising fifteen or twenty feet high, and then receded between the banks with such violence that they took whole groves of young cottonwoods with them." He moved to the next grave. "Fissures in the earth opened up and spit out sand and water, then closed up within seconds."

"It sounds fascinating. If you still have her diary, I'd love to see it," Roxana said with genuine interest.

"Sure." He shrugged. "It's at my house."

"Did your great-great-grandmother live through the earthquake?" she asked.

"Yes, but she died two years later in childbirth. My great-grandfather was raised by James's second wife. He said James told him that he had never loved his second wife with the passion that he had loved Maudie."

"Maudie? Was that her name?"

"Yes. Maude Michelle Renoir-Austin. She was French."

"Do you have any pictures of her?" Roxana inquired.

"An oil portrait that has been passed down through the generations. She had black hair like yours and big brown eyes. Her face was heart-shaped." Sonny's forefinger ran lightly along her jawline. "James Austin kidnapped her."

"Really? Why?"

"Because she didn't want to live in this wild place," he replied. "He kept her here under lock and key until she fell in love with this place and with him."

"How dramatic! It seems to me that the men around here have a tradition of kidnapping their women." Her pulse raced as Sonny bent his head and his lips brushed across hers.

"We Austins don't take no for an answer unless we're absolutely forced to," he murmured before this mouth settled on her soft and trembling lips. Sonny gathered her to him in a surge of desire. He drove his fingers through her silky hair, still damp from the lake, and heat grew in his loins until he thought he would die from wanting her.

"Roxie, Roxie," he whispered against her throat, "I've never wanted any woman more than I want you." His hands moved under her vest and he gasped with delight when he discovered that she wore nothing underneath it. He inched back enough to fill his hands with her soft, pliant breasts. His thumbs flicked across her nipples, and they puckered into points of pleasure. A strangled moan slipped past her lips, and she brought his head up for another drugging kiss.

Hot passion seared her, and Roxana tore her mouth from Sonny's and gasped for breath. He inched up the flimsy vest, and his lips closed over one straining nipple. Roxana's head jerked back as a spasm of ecstasy seized her.

"Sonny!" Her voice trembled with passion. She pushed at his shoulders, unsure of what she wanted more—to be released from this sweet torture or to succumb to her burning desire.

Sonny suddenly released her and moved away. He inhaled a head-clearing breath that didn't begin to assuage his throbbing need. He ran a hand through his hair, then rubbed the back of his neck, as if trying to massage away his frustration.

Roxana stared at Sonny's broad back. Slowly she closed the distance between them and gently caressed his quivering shoulders.

"Don't do that," he said through clenched teeth. "We'd better get back to the lodge. I've got a million things to do there."

"Sonny..." Roxana dropped her hands to her sides. "What's wrong?"

"What's wrong!" He spun around to face her. "I'm about this close to making love to you!" His thumb and forefinger moved to within an inch of each other. "And this isn't the place for that kind of activity. Come on. Let's go." He grabbed her hand and pulled her with him.

Roxana trotted to keep up with his long strides, and a peculiar sense of regret coursed through her. Did he think he was the only one on the verge of unbridled passion? Didn't he know that she wanted him so desperately that it frightened her?

Roxana watched until Sonny disappeared inside the resort; then she sighed and picked up her fishing equipment.

The boat ride back to the lodge had been fraught with a sexual tension that neither one of them had attempted to penetrate. Roxana's nerves had been too raw to make the effort, and Sonny had seemed tired and angry. She draped her sweater over her arm and struggled up the incline that led to the hotel. She could still feel his lips and hands roaming across her sensitive skin. Her stomach muscles quivered, and she felt as if she were on the verge of exploding.

She had never felt like this before, she thought. Sonny didn't even have to touch her to make her insides melt. One look from those sky-blue eyes sent her tumbling over the edge of desire.

Her steps faltered when a shadow fell across the path. Roxana looked up, and her breath caught in her throat when she recognized the woman blocking her way.

"Heather!" Roxana cried. "Well, the world of professional journalism is rather small, isn't it?"

Heather Rhodes smiled, and her green-eyed gaze took in Roxana's wrinkled appearance. "Yes, long time no see, Roxana," Heather said in a purring voice. "Have you been fishing or swimming?"

"Well...I..." Roxana looked down at her damp clothing, then back up to her former college roommate. "A little bit of both, I guess. What are you doing here?"

"Stalking wild game."

Roxana shook her head in confusion, and Heather's lips twitched into a catlike grin.

"I'm stalking Sonny Austin," Heather explained, "and I'm hoping that you will help me set a trap for him."

Six

So you do work for *Pinup* now," Roxana stated. "The last time I bumped into you, you were writing for a theater magazine. What happened?"

Heather flung out her hands in surrender. "Let's just say that *Pinup* offered me a more interesting position—and the fringe benefits are unbeatable!" She grinned seductively. "You seem to be doing well since graduation, Roxana. *Sportspeople* is perfect for you. You always were into jocks."

"I enjoy sports," Roxana amended sternly. "Does Sonny know you're here?"

Heather shrugged. "I don't know if he does or not. It's a free country. I can go where I please."

"What exactly are you doing here at Point Pleasure?" Roxana asked, shifting the heavy tackle box from one hand to the other.

"I'm working. We're doing a feature on the local angler hunks, and Sonny Austin is the *pièce de résistance.*"

"I heard that he had refused your request," Roxana noted with a slight smirk.

"We're hoping to change his mind."

"Good luck!" Roxana laughed and stepped forward. "I guess I'll see you around. I've got to get out of these smelly clothes and—"

"Wait a minute, Roxana," Heather said, placing a hand on Roxana's arm. "Is this any way to treat your old college roommate?"

"We weren't exactly bosom buddies, as I recall," Roxana reminded her. "We had only roomed together six weeks when we called it quits before we killed each other."

"It wasn't that bad," Heather admonished. "We just got on each other's nerves in close proximity."

Roxana sighed and held Heather's gaze. "What do you want, Heather? Let's drop all this nonsense and get to the crux of the matter. You didn't ambush me just to renew old acquaintances."

"I told you," Heather said, her tone less friendly now. "I'm hoping that you will help me change Sonny's mind about posing for the magazine."

"No way," Roxana said, shaking her head. "That's your problem, not mine. Keep me out of it, please."

"Roxana!" Heather's green eyes narrowed in annoyance. "I've been watching you since you arrived, and you seem to have become quite chummy with Sonny. Now, I need help. This assignment means a lot to me, and if anyone can persuade Sonny to pose for *Pinup*, I think you can."

"And *my* assignment is important to *me*," Roxana said angrily. "I'm not going to wreck it by sticking my nose into business that doesn't concern me." She looked toward the resort hotel, anxious to shake free of Heather's grip. "I've really got to go, Heather. Good luck. It was nice seeing you again."

"I'll be in touch," Heather said, letting go of Roxana's arm. "I'm dying to hear about your recent interest in angling."

Roxana stared straight ahead and hurried along the path. Heather's parting remark reverberated within her, making her feel hollow and cold. Didn't she have enough problems without Heather adding to them? With luck she would be able to avoid Heather Rhodes altogether.

Sitting on a tree stump near the bank, Roxana searched the nearby area for anything that slithered. Satisfied that she was alone in her secluded spot, she picked up her rod and reel and practiced casting, congratulating herself when she managed to feed out the line without tangling it in tree branches or snagging it in her hair.

After three days of practicing in private, she felt more confident and more prepared for her next fishing session with Sonny. Her luck was holding out, and she was beginning to think that all her misgivings were mere straws in the wind. Sonny had been kept busy with last-minute tournament details, giving Roxana time to sneak off and indulge in private fishing lessons. Armed with her instruction booklets, she had found this secluded spot about a half-mile from the resort. The hours of practice had erased much of her ineptness, but she had yet to catch a fish.

Settling more comfortably on the stump, she held the rod in one hand and rested her chin in the other, her gaze fixed on the red-and-white bobbing ball.

She missed Sonny, she thought with a wistful sigh. She had seen him only briefly during the past few days. He had stopped by her room yesterday, but had stayed only long enough to loan her Maudie's diary. She had stayed up late last night reading it. What a find! It was a fascinating history of those turbulent times and had fertilized her idea to write a novel about the area in the early 1800s or, at the very least, a nonfiction book incorporating the numerous legends of Reelfoot and its people. Could she write such a book and continue her work with *Sportspeople*? she wondered. Would she be able to find the time to write it while still holding down a demanding job as a reporter?

Roxana laughed softly at her own musings, thinking that she was putting the cart before the horse. It was rather lofty thinking on her part to be so confident that she could actually write a book, nonfiction or fiction; however, the prospect excited her, and the challenge of such an endeavor made her itch to try it.

As she looked out at the gently lapping lake, contentment stole through her. Never in her wildest dreams had she imagined that she would feel so at home here. There was something about this place that appealed to her and made her want to enjoy every moment.

But was it Reelfoot Lake or Sonny Austin that really appealed to her? Was she merely fooling herself by thinking that it was the lake and not the man who made her want to stay forever? Maybe the notion of writing a book was just a convenient excuse to return to this place. Roxana sighed away her soul-searching thoughts, preferring not to examine her motives too carefully.

As she gazed up at the robin's-egg-blue sky, Roxana's thoughts moved lazily to the man who was so firmly rooted in this place. How long could she hope to fool Sonny into thinking that she was an expert angler? Oh, sure, she had improved during the past few days, but not enough to hoodwink Sonny. When this house of cards fell around her, would Sonny understand her motives?

She moaned softly and closed her eyes as her mind flashed the memory of Sonny's touching retelling of his heartache when he discovered Sarah's penchant for lying. Was this assignment important enough to risk the chance of hurting him again? she wondered.

The temptation to confess surged through her, but she squelched it. How could she escape the trap she was setting for herself? Maybe she could pretend to be ill or sprain her ankle or wrist or...

Roxana rejected the options, realizing that removing herself from the competition would only result in Sonny being unable to compete. The tournament was important to him, and she couldn't withdraw and deny him the opportunity to compete in his own contest of skill.

Shaking off her gloomy thoughts, Roxana reeled in her line and stood up. Mentally reviewing the instructions on how to cast, she took aim at a spot a few yards from the bank and pressed the trigger.

Her timing was off, and the line fed out behind her back.

"Oh, fiddlesticks!" Roxana untangled the line behind her and cranked it in. "I'll never learn how to do this!"

"Never say never, Roxana."

Roxana whirled in the direction of the purring voice. Heather stepped out from the shadows, a knowing smile curving her full lips. She pushed a pair of tortoiseshell sunglasses to the top of her head, her green eyes sparkling with triumph.

"How long have you been spying on me?" Roxana demanded.

"I didn't need to spy, Roxana. I've heard from a dotty old gentleman called General Tee that you are a top-notch angler. I've kept your little secret."

"What secret?" Roxana asked fearfully.

"Roxana, don't try to kid a kidder," Heather scolded. "We might have roomed together for only a few weeks, but I can read you like a book. You love sports as a spectator, not as a participant. If you're an expert angler, then I'm a Pulitzer Prize winner."

"If you have dreams of winning a Pulitzer Prize, then you'd better resign from *Pinup*," Roxana said with a haughty smile. "That's not exactly what one would call laudable journalism."

Heather moved around the tree stump and sat on it. A great beauty in college, she was still stunning, with her russet-colored hair flowing around her shoulders and her very expressive almond-shaped eyes. She plucked a blade of grass from the leg of her brushed-denim trousers, then rolled up the sleeves of her blue Oxford shirt.

"Are you going to tell me why you're following me?" Roxana asked, quickly losing patience with Heather's calculated preening.

"I wanted to observe your technique," Heather said. "I've heard so much about your fishing talent that I just had to see it for myself."

Roxana dropped to the carpet of grass. "Okay, so I can't fish. So what?"

"So why did you tell everyone that you could?"

"Because Sonny Austin wanted to be interviewed by a reporter who knew about fishing. Things have gotten out of control, but it's nothing serious," Roxana said, hearing the false ring to her words.

"You're his fishing partner in this tournament, and you can't even cast, and you don't think that's serious?"

"I can cast!" Roxana grabbed the rod and reel, stood up, and to her own amazement, reeled out the line like a true professional. "There! Are you satisfied?"

"You're still saturated with beginner's luck, aren't you?" Heather shook her head and laughed lightly. "Even back in college you could always fly through sticky situations on a wing and a prayer."

"Luck had nothing to do with it." Roxana winced, realizing how easily lies were springing to her lips these days. "Oh, Heather!" She plopped herself down on the grass again with a weary sigh. "I have enough problems without your adding to them."

Heather regarded her for a few tense moments before she stuck out one hand and smiled. "Truce?"

Roxana shook her hand. "Truce."

Heather breathed a sigh of relief. "Ah! That feels better. I don't want to spar with you, Roxana. Why should we behave like enemies when we're both in the same leaky boat?"

"What do you mean?" Roxana asked with curiosity.

"My assignment is as important to me as yours is to you," Heather explained. "If I can get Sonny to pose for the magazine, it will mean a promotion for me and a raise in pay I desperately need."

"You aren't in financial trouble, are you?" Roxana asked with concern.

"Not really. I've fallen in love with a house in Hermosa Beach. I can't handle the payments on my present salary without a lot of sacrificing, but if I get a raise, I can swing it with no problem." Heather rested her chin in her hands and stared moodily out at the lake. "You should see it. It's a whitewashed cottage with pink shutters. Oh, I could be so happy there."

"Where are you living now?"

"In a cramped apartment in Los Angeles with three other women. It's terrible! You know how I've always treasured my privacy. That's why I went through roommates like a fashion model goes through fad diets."

Roxana nodded, remembering how impossible it had been to live with Heather. "This assignment means a promotion for me, too. It's my first cover story, and all this deceit is my editor's brainstorm."

"Editors are like generals. They issue impossible commands and expect their troops to come through with flying colors, no matter what," Heather complained.

"You said it!" Roxana looked at the lake's smooth surface, then suddenly jumped to her feet. "My floater is gone! I've hooked something!" She reeled in the line, feeling the resistance. "Oh, Heather! I've really got something! No kidding!"

Heather rose to her feet and clapped her hands. "Reel it in! Hurry!"

Roxana cranked the line in. Whatever was on the other end was big. The flexible rod bowed, and the reel groaned and complained as Roxana struggled to land her catch.

"It's a tree limb," Heather said, laughing.

"No, it's a big..." Roxana stared at the limb floating to the surface. "Tree limb," she finished with a groan.

"Here, let me help untangle the line," Heather said, moving to the edge of the bank and reaching out for the limb. She yanked it closer to her and removed the hook from the bark. "There you go."

"Thanks. I wonder if you can win a fishing tournament by catching the biggest tree limb."

"I don't think they count anything you can't eat." Heather sat on the tree stump again. "How long do you think you can pull the wool over Sonny's eyes?"

"Your guess is as good as mine," Roxana admitted, placing the rod and reel to one side and sitting again on the soft grass. "Sometimes I think I can keep up the farce, and other times I'm sure I'm on the verge of making a fool of myself."

"Roxana, could you try to talk Sonny into agreeing to do the photo layout for me?" Heather asked, a note of desperation tinging her voice.

"He won't agree, and I'm certainly not in any position to change his mind about anything," Roxana said, meeting Heather's pleading gaze. "I'd like to help you, Heather, but I can't. It takes every bit of concentration I can muster to keep myself afloat. Don't you understand?"

"Yes, I guess so." Heather squared her shoulders and sighed. "I wish he wouldn't make a federal case out of this! What's the big deal about flaunting his obvious attributes?"

"He's modest," Roxana explained. "I wouldn't pose nude for a magazine, either. Would you?"

Heather grinned. "Not on your life!"

"So, why should Sonny be any different?"

"Hey, whose side are you on?" Heather cried.

Roxana hugged her knees and laughed. "Let's just say I'm impartial." She looked at Heather. "You aren't going to blow the whistle on me, are you?"

"No. Will you at least consider talking to Sonny about the photo layout? I mean, if the subject comes up, will you try to get him to see my side of it?"

"If the subject comes up I'll put in a good word for you," Roxana promised.

"Thanks." Heather stuck up her thumb in a jaunty salute. "Hope your luck holds out, Roxana."

"So do I. Where are you staying?"

"In a guest cottage at the other end of the lake," Heather replied, raising herself off the stump.

"Are you going to talk to Sonny again about the photo session?" Roxana ssked.

"Yes, but I'm biding my time. We're busy snapping other anglers right now and—"

"Anyone I know?" Roxana interrupted, giving in to her curiosity.

Heather shook her head. "Most of them are college students who fish on weekends; however, I'm close to talking Tim Duncan into posing for us."

"The football player?"

"Yes. He's entered in this tournament," Heather explained. "I was hoping Sonny might reconsider if Tim agrees."

"He might." Roxana shrugged, knowing without a doubt that Tim's decision wouldn't sway Sonny one inch.

"The pictures are very tasteful, and our photographers are some of the best in the—"

"You don't have to sell me, Heather," Roxana said with a grin. "Not unless you're asking me to pose."

Heather lifted her brows. "You never know.... Maybe Sonny would agree to a photo if you were in it, too!"

"Forget it!"

Heather laughed and waved one hand. "I'll see you around, Roxana. I hope the next thing you catch has scales and fins."

"Thanks, loads, smart mouth. 'Bye!" Roxana waved, then turned back to the lake. With a heavy sigh she picked up the rod and reel to resume her practice session. She had promised to meet Sonny tomorrow morning for another fishing trip, and that didn't leave much time to polish up her pitiful act. Sonny was more intelligent than Heather in many ways, and she hadn't fooled Heather for one second!

"What's the name of this place?" Roxana asked when Sonny stopped the bass boat in a shady pocket.

"Eagle Nest Timber."

"Are there eagles here?"

"Sometimes." He opened his tackle box and rummaged through it for a yellow-and-red crappie jig. His gaze fell on her own fishing pole, and he frowned. "Are you going to use a floater?"

"Yes. Why?" Roxana moved the red-and-white ball higher up on the line.

"It's hard to catch crappie with a floater."

"You think so?" she asked, carefully phrasing the question.

"Yes. Crappie have paper mouths," he explained. "You can barely feel them when they hit your line, and by the time your floater bobs, it's too late."

"Too late," Roxana echoed, struggling to understand his explanation. Too late for what? she wondered.

"Yes, they're long gone by the time your bobber moves."

"Well, I've had pretty good luck so far and—"

"Why not give it a try without the floater?" Sonny insisted.

"Okay." Roxana removed the plastic ball. "I'm game." She held her breath and flicked the rod. The line fed out, and the lure fell a few feet from the bank. Roxana released her pent-up breath and thanked her lucky stars for small favors.

"Here goes nothing," Sonny said, casting out his line with admirable ease. "What have you been doing the past few days?" he asked.

"Reading that diary you loaned me."

"Was it interesting?"

"Fascinating. It's given me some ideas," she said.

"About what?" Sonny asked, easing himself down into one of the chairs.

"About writing a book...maybe." She glanced at him and caught his smile. "What do you think about that?"

"Sounds great to me. Lord knows there's plenty of material around these parts for a good yarn."

"What have you been doing?" she asked Sonny.

"Working my tail off." He sighed wearily, aiming his expelled breath upward so that it lifted the straight blond hair off his forehead. "I think we're ready for the tournament now. I know *I'm* ready for it."

Roxana sat in the other chair, keeping her own counsel. She would never be ready for the tournament, but she was anxious to get it over with. A burden would be lifted from her shoulders when this stupid contest was over and done with!

"Uh...Roxie?" Sonny said, interrupting her reverie.

"Yes?" She glanced at him, and he nodded toward the water.

"I think you have a bite," he said.

Her gaze flew to the quivering line. "Oh, my gosh!"

"Use the reel this time, okay?"

"Right, right!" She reeled in the line, excitement making her hands shake. Standing up, she balanced herself precariously in the swaying boat and reeled in the last few feet of line. To her utter surprise and relief there was actually a fish at the end of it. "Look at that!" she announced.

"Nice little crappie," Sonny said, grabbing the squirming fish. "Want me to take it off the hook for you?"

"Yes, thanks." Thank you from the bottom of my squeamish little heart, she mentally added while he plucked the hook from the fish's mouth.

Sonny tested the weight of the white fish in his hand. "About a half-pounder, I'd say. Not bad." He leaned over and dropped the fish into the water. "Send up your big brother, pal."

"What are you doing?" Roxana curbed her temper, although she would have loved to slug Sonny Austin. "Why did you let it go?"

He threw her a baffled look. "Why did you want to keep it?"

"Well...I..." She shook her head, realizing that she couldn't tell him she had wanted to keep the fish because it was the first one she had ever caught. "I thought we might have a fish fry tonight, that's all," she explained.

He cocked one eyebrow. "Right, but we'll catch bigger ones than that before the day is over."

Sonny sat down and picked up his rod again. He was silent for a few moments; then he snapped his fingers. "Hey, I almost forgot. I've got something for you."

"What?" Roxana asked, wondering what kind of curve he was getting ready to throw her as she cast out her line again without difficulty.

"This." He opened his tackle box and pulled out a white hat with a black bill, turning it around for her to read the words printed across the front: CATCH OF THE DAY.

Roxana laughed. "How thoughtful of you."

"It's appropriate, don't you think? You're about the best thing I've hauled out of these waters in a long, long time." He fitted the hat on her head, then leaned back to get a good look at her. "You're as cute as a button in that, Roxie." He kissed her lips in a friendly gesture. "And you've got another bite."

She whipped her head around and began reeling in the taut line. "I don't believe this!"

"Me either. You sure are a show-off this morning." Sonny reached for the net and leaned over the side of the boat. "Hold it right there, and I'll net it." He captured the fish and held it up for her inspection. "Look at this! This is a keeper, honey."

He removed the hook with his pliers, opened the boat's well and dropped the fish down into it. "Just swim around there for a while, buddy. I'll get back to you." He let the lid bang shut, then retrieved his rod and reel. "Looks like you're going to catch all the fish today. I haven't even had a nibble. Wait a second...." His hands tightened on the rod, and he narrowed his eyes in intense concentration. "I think something is messing with my line."

"Reel it in!" Roxana cried.

"It hasn't bit yet; it's just teasing me."

Keeping an eye on his progress, Roxana flicked her rod and met with disaster when the line fed out behind her instead of in front of her.

"Hey, hey!" Sonny grabbed at the collar of his shirt. "You've hooked me, doggone it!" He cursed viciously under his breath and dropped his rod in disgust. "You made me lose that fish!"

"Oh, I'm sorry," Roxana said, not knowing how to smooth his ruffled feathers.

Sonny yanked his collar around until he could see it, then plucked the hook from the material. "I swear, sometimes you act like a rank amateur, Roxana!"

She knew he was really ticked off when he used her given name instead of her nickname. Roxana threw her rod and reel down, crossed her arms under her breasts and swiveled her chair around, turning her back to him.

"What's wrong now?" Sonny asked belligerently.

"I'm tired. I don't want to fish anymore."

"Well, I'm not tired." Sonny reeled in his line, then cast it out again. "You're not tired, either; you're just pouting."

"I'm tired!" Roxana argued, daring him to contradict her.

He shrugged and focused his attention on the shimmering line that stretched out before him. "You need to take vitamins if this little dab of activity tuckers you out."

Roxana made a face at his back, then turned aside and stared gloomily at a speedboat in the hazy distance. The sun was well up in the sky, heading toward its zenith and heating up the still air. She wasn't pouting or angry. She was just too chicken to try casting again. One fiasco was enough for the day. Sonny had hit the nail on the head with his biting observation. She couldn't flirt with disaster. It would be safer if she let him think she was pouting because he had yelled at her.

"Got one!" Sonny reeled in a crappie and placed it in the well. "Are you just going to sit there like a bump on a log?"

"Yes," she answered sarcastically.

"Suit yourself." He fed out the line again, and it no sooner hit the surface before he was reeling it in with a joyous whoop. "Got another one! Don't that beat all?"

Much to Roxana's irritation, Sonny caught six more crappie in the next hour. Each time his line quivered, he whooped and hollered and teased her for giving up so soon. When he started to reel out his line after the sixth fish had been dumped into the well, Roxana reached out a hand to stop him.

"Sonny, I'm hungry," she said.

"I can remedy that," he said, nodding toward a wicker basket. "I brought us a picnic lunch. Help yourself." He grinned, looking happy and carefree. "These fish will top off the tournament fish fry tonight."

"I thought we were going to have a private fish fry," she said, her voice heavy with disappointment.

He threw her a helpless look. "I have to be there, Roxie. I'm the host."

She nodded in agreement. So much for getting him alone for the evening.

"We could leave a little early and go to my place for a nightcap," Sonny suggested.

Roxana smiled. "You won't have to twist my arm." She glanced at the wicker basket. "Why don't we have lunch on the bank? It looks lovely and cool over there under those willow trees."

"My pleasure." Sonny sighed and stowed away his rod and reel. "The fish will stop biting anyway, now that it's getting close to noon."

"You don't mind? I didn't have breakfast and I'm—"

He shook his head, cutting off her sentence. "I don't mind a bit. Sharing a picnic lunch with you is no hardship, believe me. We can eat lunch and...relax." He grinned and wiggled his eyebrows lasciviously.

"I can use the time to interview you," Roxana suggested cheerily.

A frown touched the corners of his mouth. "That's not what I had in mind—" he yanked violently on the starter cord, and the motor roared, drowning out his bitter "—and you damn well know it!"

Seven

"Why did I become interested in the elderly and the handicapped?" Sonny said, repeating the question Roxana had posed. He stretched out on his side on the red blanket and propped himself on one elbow. Gazing up, he watched a flock of black birds soar across a clear blue sky. A cypress spread its limbs above him, splashing the ground with shade and dappled sunlight. What a gorgeous day, he thought, then switched his gaze from the blue canopy to Roxana's eyes. She looked younger than springtime in her white overalls and red T-shirt, and he wished she would put aside that infernal tape recorder and make love to him.

"That's the question," Roxana said. "Got an answer?"

"Not really." He took a sip of cola from the can he held in one hand. "I've always been aware of the elderly and the handicapped. It wasn't like I woke up one morning and said, 'Hey! I'm going to be nice to senior citizens and those less fortunate than me!' Fishing is something everybody can do; I started holding clinics for specialized groups, that's all."

Roxana reached out and touched his knee. "I think it's sweet of you to help others." Her voice was slightly huskier than usual.

"And I think you have the sexiest voice I've ever heard," Sonny said, reaching out to grab her hand before she could remove it from his knee. "How did you get that voice, anyway?"

"I was born with it," Roxana said with a little laugh. "My mother thought I had a cold all winter long, until the doctor told her that I would always sound a little hoarse. When I *do* have a cold, all I can do is squeak. I sound like Minnie Mouse."

"There is so much about you that I want to know," he whispered, pulling her hand to his chest. "So much I want to discover."

Roxana switched off the tape recorder and laughed softly. "I don't think we need to put this on tape. You know, I have a few more questions...."

"So do I, but I don't want them taped."

Questions? Roxana stiffened slightly and felt her nerves flutter. Was this it? Was he going to ask her why she had lied to him about being able to fish?

Feeling her uneasiness, Sonny lifted her fingers to his lips and kissed them, one by one. "Do you like the lake?" he asked.

"Is that one of the questions?"

"Yes."

Relief poured through her, and she relaxed. "I love the lake," she replied softly.

"Don't you think it's about the prettiest lake you've ever seen?"

"Yes." She quivered when his lips pressed into the palm of her hand. "Can we continue the interview?"

"Don't you have enough for now?" he asked, glancing at the tape recorder. "You've asked me hundreds of questions."

"More like a dozen or so," she corrected, but didn't press. She gently removed her hand from his and sat up on her knees. "Now what? Do you have to get back to the resort or—"

"Or," he said, grabbing her by the wrists and pulling her down on top of him. "We've had lunch. Now let's have dessert." His lips brushed across hers. "Sweeter than sugar, that's what you are. Do you know how much I enjoy being near you? You're special, Roxie." His lips touched her earlobe; then this teeth nipped it lightly. "You make me want to take a chance again."

"Take a chance on what?" Roxana asked.

"On falling in love again."

Her heart slammed against her chest. Could this be happening? Was he just saying what she wanted to hear, or was he serious? She raised her head to look down into his incredibly blue eyes. His smile warmed the corners of her soul and made her blood sing.

"Why are you looking at me like that?" he asked with a little chuckle."

"Like what?"

"Like you think I'm being less than truthful."
He lifted his head off the blanket and touched her
lips with his. "I would never lie to you, honey.
You're the first woman I've wanted to take a chance
with since Sarah. Believe me?"

Contradictory feelings warred within her. Joy
was overshadowed by shame, truth by deceit. "I
believe you, but maybe we shouldn't be too hasty.
I mean, where could this lead? You live here, and I
live in New York. Do you think a long-distance
romance has a chance?"

"It wouldn't have to be long distance," he reminded her.

Roxana stretched her body out beside him. "You
mean you'd move to New York?" she asked
incredulously.

"Well, I was thinking that since you love the
lake, you'd move here."

"You have conveniently forgotten that *Sportspeople* is headquartered in Manhattan," she said.

He removed her hat and flung it aside to see her
face better. "You could write your book here and
forget that magazine."

"Just like that, huh?" She stared at the black
fringe on the blanket as resentment reared its head.

"Why not?" he asked.

Roxana pushed herself up. Sitting cross-legged,
she pinned him with dark eyes. "Why don't you
give up your job and relocate to New York?"

"That's ridiculous!" He propped himself up on
his elbows.

"That's ridiculous, but it makes perfect sense
that I should give up my job and relocate? Begging
your pardon, sir, but isn't that a bit chauvinistic?"

His head dropped back, and exasperation played across his face. "Here we go! There's nothing worse than a women's libber spouting off about—"

"Hold on a minute, buster!" Roxana poked a finger into his shoulder. "Don't say something that will make me despise you. You might think that fishing is more important than journalism, but that's your problem."

"I didn't say that," he fumed, piercing her with a sharp glare. "All I'm saying is that it's easier for you to relocate than it is for me. There aren't any crappie in Manhattan!"

"That's true. Somehow we've managed to live without them."

"How did we get on this subject, anyway?" he asked, and threw his arms up in wonder.

"You started weaving dreams of how I would give up everything I've worked for to come here to fish and write books that no one has shown an interest in yet."

"Don't you think you could write a novel and sell it?" he asked her.

"It's not as easy as reeling in a fish," she answered.

"You know I do more than just catch fish!" He sat up, leaning his forearms against his bent knees. "I happen to own and operate a resort. I'm also an author." His blue eyes flashed fire. "I've written four books on fishing. If I can sell a book, I imagine you can, too. After all, you're a writer. I'm just a dim-witted country boy with a yen for fishing."

Realizing that she had insulted him, she placed a hand on his shoulder and winced when he pulled away from her. "Sonny, I'm sorry," she whispered. "You know I don't think of you in those terms. You're the most wonderful man I've ever known."

He stared straight ahead for several seconds, then turned to face her. "Then why are we fighting?"

"I don't know. I guess we're trying to sort all this out and come up with a simple solution."

"It's too pretty a day to waste fussing and fuming with each other." He lifted a hand and ran his fingers through her hair. "Kiss me, Roxie. Kiss me."

She leaned forward until her mouth rested on his. His fingers gathered her hair, making her scalp tingle. He parted her lips and invaded her warm mouth with his tongue.

"That's better," he mumbled as his mouth traveled down her cheek to the side of her neck. "This is the way to spend a lazy afternoon."

"Sonny?" Roxana murmured.

"Hmmm?" He nuzzled her neck, and the tip of his tongue moistened her skin.

"Have you...have you been in love with anyone since Sarah?"

Seconds ticked by before he finally answered. "No. I haven't wanted anyone until now." He lifted his head and looked straight into her eyes with an honesty that pierced her heart. "It took me until now to get over her, I guess. But I *am* over her, Roxie. You've made me want to love again...to trust again."

She closed her eyes, and his lips reclaimed hers in a sweet kiss. The contradictions swirled within her again, making the moment bittersweet. She was falling in love with him, but the realization brought pain as well as pleasure. What would he do when he discovered that she was a bigger cheat than Sarah?

Laughter and animated chatter filled the evening air, and the aroma of frying fish lingered. Roxana moved to a secluded spot beneath a sheltering elm and watched as the tournament guests consumed crappie, catfish, hush puppies and French fries. Beer flowed from huge kegs, and pitchers of iced tea and lemonade were passed from table to table.

She had tasted her first crappie and had made a glutton of herself. The sweet-tasting, tender meat had been a pleasant surprise, and the hush puppies had melted in her mouth.

Her hunger sated and her psyche at peace, she leaned against the tree trunk and let the good times wash over her. With loving eyes she watched as Sonny moved from one guest to another, leaving smiles in his wake. Tables had been placed on the wide lawn in front of the hotel for the old-fashioned fish fry, and colored lanterns provided soft light. Sonny stopped by General Tee's table and listened while the elderly man related a tall tale.

Roxana's gaze moved slowly over him, and yearning wafted through her body. Tan, front-pleated trousers and a long-sleeved, brown-checked shirt that was open at the throat lent him an aura of casual sophistication and reminded Roxana of the first time she had seen him. He had been wearing a suit then, and she had thought he looked more like a businessman than a sportsman. Tonight he was mixing business with pleasure by hosting this dinner party and by taking time to welcome his guests and wish them good luck in the tournament, which would begin Monday. Fifty-six people had entered the event, many of them celebrities of some sort. The informal fish fry was the perfect way to let the celebrities and the professional fishermen stand on equal footing.

"Just like a journalist," Tim Duncan said as he approached Roxana. "Standing here, taking it all in, instead of being part of it all." He shook a scolding finger at her. "You should let your hair down and get with it, Roxana."

"I'm taking a breather." She shook her head when he offered her a cigarette. "I heard through the grapevine that you might bare all for a popular magazine."

His eyebrows shot up, and he expelled a long stream of smoke. "Word gets around fast, doesn't it?"

"So it's true?" she asked.

"Why not?" He shrugged and took another drag on the cigarette. "They're making me an offer I don't intend to refuse. I never knew those things paid so well!"

"You don't think you'll be a little uncomfortable posing in the nude?"

"I don't have anything to be ashamed of. I think it's kind of flattering," he said with a smile. "Besides, I have only a few years left in pro football, so I think I'd better till the soil while the sun still shines."

"I suppose it could be fun being a sex symbol," she admitted.

He laughed and shook his head. "That'll be the day! Are you ready for the tournament?"

"As ready as I'll ever be, I guess."

"General Tee is chomping at the bit. He's determined to whip Sonny this year. He's really a character. He thinks that fishing is better than sex."

"Oh, come on," Roxana scoffed. "Nothing's better than sex."

Tim leaned closer to her in a show of conspiracy. "Don't tell General Tee that unless you want a fight on your hands." He straightened, took another drag on his cigarette, then threw it down and ground it into the soft earth with the heel of his shoe. "I heard that Sonny might be the centerfold in that magazine we were discussing," he casually mentioned.

"Oh, I don't think that Sonny would—"

"Would what?"

Tim whirled around to face Sonny, and Roxana jumped slightly. Where had he come from? she wondered.

"We were talking about *Pinup* magazine," Tim explained, clamping a hand on Sonny's shoulder. "I've agreed to strut my stuff for them, and I heard that you might do the same."

"No way!" Sonny's lips twisted in a frown of disgust. "They've been after me, but they're barking up the wrong tree."

"Good." Tim laughed and shook Sonny's shoulder playfully. "I wouldn't want you showing me up. I want all the spotlight."

"It's all yours, Duncan," Sonny assured him. "Oh, General Tee is looking for you. He wants you to vouch for the one-that-got-away story he's telling."

"I can't let my partner down. See you two later."
Tim headed toward General Tee's table.

Sonny stepped closer to Roxana and grasped her
elbow. "I've fulfilled my duties as host. How about
coming back to my place with me and seeing my
etchings?"

"Don't you want to stay and hear General Tee's
exciting story?" Roxana asked.

"Not particularly." Sonny's arm encircled her
waist as they hurried along the walkway to his
house. "His stories are about as exciting as watching a bucket of hair."

Roxana laughed at his homespun humor. "I love
the way you talk."

"Is that all you love about me?"

"That's enough for starters. I don't want to give
you a big head," she said. She glanced at him
through the filtering moonlight. If she began list-
ing the things she loved about him, it would take all
night, and she was hoping for more sensuous
activities.

Sonny opened the front door and had no sooner
closed it behind them when he gathered Roxana in
his arms and kissed her passionately.

"I've been wanting to do that all evening," he
whispered, his lips brushing across her hair.

"Why didn't you?" Roxana asked, letting her
fingers comb through his silky hair.

"When it comes to loving, I like mine private."
He released her and switched on a table lamp. "I
can't believe that Duncan is really going to let those
people take pictures of him."

"Some people don't see anything wrong with it."
She moved across the living room and sat on the

couch. "As a matter of fact, I can think of a lot of other things that are more unpleasant."

"You approve of those magazines?" he asked, sitting beside her. "Would you let someone photograph you in your altogether?"

"No." Roxana dropped her gaze. "But I don't think any less of Tim for considering it."

"I don't hold it against him, but I think he's crazy. The real crazies, though, are the people who work for that magazine. That reporter I told you about from *Pinup* followed me here."

Roxana busied herself with removing her loafers, and Sonny stood up and went over to the portable bar in the corner of the living room.

"What do you want to drink?" he asked.

"Do you have any wine?"

"I've got a good bottle of dry California wine. How does that sound?"

"Tasty." She curled her legs up under her. "Has the reporter from *Pinup* contacted you?"

"Not yet, but I'm sure she'll get around to it."

Should she tell him that she knew Heather? Roxana wondered. Wouldn't it be better if he heard it from her instead of from someone else?

"Here you go," he said, handing her one of the glasses he held. "To golden days and velvet nights." He touched his glass to hers and smiled.

"I'll drink to that," Roxana said. "You know, you shouldn't be too hard on that reporter. She's only doing her job."

Sonny dropped to the couch in a lazy sprawl. "What a job! Reporters are nothing but vultures."

"You don't mean that," Roxana admonished.

His eyes widened as if he had just heard his own words. "I didn't mean to place you in that category. You're different, Roxie. You have...integrity."

If he had slapped her, it wouldn't have stung her more. Roxana retreated, feeling wounded and exposed. She gulped at the wine, then set the glass on the table. Her transgressions fell upon her like stinging wasps, and she shot up from the couch, mindless of everything other than her need to escape the assault.

"Where are you going?" Sonny sat up and grasped her wrist.

"I...it's late," she said.

"But it's only ten."

"It is?" She looked around in confusion. Where could she run to? How could she untangle herself from this web she had spun? "I...I should go back to my room."

"No, you shouldn't," Sonny said as he stood up to block her way. He shook his head in stern, stubborn refusal.

"Sonny, I can't stay. I have to—"

"Roxie, you *must* stay." His lips grazed her temple, and his hands framed her face. "Don't be afraid of me. I won't hurt you."

"I know." She closed her eyes, and a helpless whimper slipped past her lips. "I'm not afraid...of you."

He buried his face in her hair and breathed in deeply. "You smell wonderful," he said. His thumbs moved across her cheeks. "You feel wonderful. I won't let you go this time, Roxie. Put your arms around me."

She slipped her arms around his waist and held him fast.

"Can you feel me trembling?" he whispered intimately. "I haven't done that in such a long, long time. I want...oh, I want!"

"What?" Roxana asked, barely getting the word past her lips.

"I want to explore every inch of you." He drew back, and his fingers moved to unbutton the front of her blouse. "You have the most beautiful body."

He parted her blouse, holding out the fabric as his lambent gaze licked across her lace-covered breasts and set her afire. Pushing the blouse off her smooth shoulders, he let it drop to the floor. "Your breasts are so lovely," he whispered, unhooking her bra and letting it join her blouse. "So full and soft." His hands cupped them, and his thumbs flicked across their centers until she trembled and moaned.

When he bent his head and kissed one taut bud, Roxana hooked her thumbs in his belt to keep from falling to the floor in a heap of longing. His lips parted to take her inside his warm mouth, his tongue exploring her and his teeth nipping her until she cried out in sweet agony.

"Sonny...Sonny...I want you. Heaven help me, but I do." The admission sprang to her lips before her mind could register the words.

Sonny's arms came around her, and he lifted her into the cradle of his embrace and mounted the stairs to his loft bedroom. His mouth closed over hers in a kiss that sent shudders of desire through her. He placed her on the bed, kicked off his shoes, then snuggled into her waiting embrace. Roxana pulled his shirt free of his waistband and slipped her hands beneath it. His skin was warm and vibrant, and she wanted to touch him all over.

His lips returned to her breasts, sucking and nuzzling and driving her wild. Her hands moved restlessly across his back, and she arched her body into his in an age-old appeal for fulfillment. She parted her legs, and Sonny slipped between them. He pressed into her, and she felt him, hard and straining for release.

Moving down her body, he rained kisses across her stomach while he unsnapped her slacks and eased down the zipper. She lifted her hips, helping him remove her remaining clothes. He tossed them into a chair, then started to unbutton his shirt.

"No," Roxana said, sitting up and facing him. "Let me." She unbuttoned his shirt and pushed it off his shoulders and down his muscled arms. So strong and virile, she thought as her fingers unhooked his belt and then his trousers.

He stood and swiftly removed the rest of his clothing as if he couldn't bear another moment of her agonizing pace. Roxana stared at him in unabashed fascination. His body was solid and covered with a forest of reddish-gold hair. Long muscles flexed in his thighs and rippled along his flat stomach. He didn't carry an ounce of extra weight, not even around his middle.

"I knew the first time I saw you that all you wanted was to see me with my clothes off," he said with a rakish smile.

Roxana laughed and held out her arms. "That's not all I wanted, Mr. Austin," she said playfully.

Placing a knee on the bed, he leaned into her, making her fall back in ready surrender. Sonny lightly ran his hand from her shoulder across her left breast, then down her smooth belly and along the inside of her thigh. She gasped, but he continued his wandering exploration. His hand moved up without hesitation, and he found the damp vestibule of her femininity. She arched, pushing into his eager hand, and vertigo overtook him. He bowed his head and kissed her inner thighs while his hands moved up to gently massage her firm breasts.

The tremors intensified until they made her quake with longing. Roxana moved restlessly beneath him as fissures of emotion opened within her and passion erupted in hot spurts. A sheen of perspiration covered her body as the firestorm overtook her. She grabbed his head and brought his lips to hers. Her tongue swept into his mouth, urgent and bold in its quest. Sonny moaned and cradled her in his arms. His body felt like a rough, warm blanket on her soft skin, and his chest hair added just the right friction against her sensitive breasts.

She tore her mouth from his and gazed longingly into his glazed eyes. "Love me, Sonny. Please love me," she whispered with urgency.

"I will...I want to...." He slipped into her so easily that Roxana's eyes widened in surprise. Sonny grinned and kissed her parted lips. "Perfect fit, love. I knew it would be."

Yes, it was perfect, Roxana thought, enjoying the sensation of having him inside her. She didn't think it could feel any better until he began to move, shattering her foolish notion. The driving invasion created shock waves within her, and she felt her body respond instinctively by clutching him and holding him in a heated embrace. Sonny threw back his head and lifted himself on stiffened arms. Cords ran down his neck, straining against his moist skin. He closed his eyes as a seizure of desire passed through him. Roxana's own lashes floated down, and the earth trembled around her.

He plunged deeper, as if trying to touch her shimmering soul. She wrapped her legs around his hips, and Sonny opened his eyes to stare in wonder at the ecstasy that played across her face. Her lips parted, but no words were uttered. He bent his head and ran his tongue across her lips before dipping it inside and tasting her sweetness. Fire flamed in his loins until its intensity could no longer be ignored. Passion conquered him, laying to waste his unselfish desire to bring her to that lofty place before him. Mindlessly he gave himself up to desire, and hoarse cries broke loose from the very center of him.

His sounds of pleasure prompted Roxana's own cries of joy. She wrapped her arms tightly around his neck and let him carry her up to a plateau of shuddering release. Slowly she drifted back to reality on the wings of fulfillment.

Sonny collapsed beside her and laughed lightly.

"What is it?" Roxana asked, propping her chin on his chest.

"Happiness," he answered simply as his arms encircled her. "I've never been this happy before, and I owe it all to you." His eyes smoldered with blue fire and smoke. "Oh, Roxana! You delight me. You bewitch me. You bewilder me."

"Bewilder?" She inched up until her lips were poised above his. "After this you're still bewildered?"

"A little. Did I disappoint you or—"

Roxana gave him a scolding frown, then kissed him. "Men! The more macho you seem, the more insecure you are!" She laughed and kissed him again. "If it had been any better, I wouldn't have survived. There! Are you satisfied?"

"No." His arms tightened around her waist. "But I will be by sunrise. Temporarily, at least." He silenced her husky laughter with a kiss that left no room for doubt.

Roxana bolted upright. "Hey! Did you just slap me across my bottom, or was I having a nightmare?"

"Good morning!" Sonny beamed at her. "Get that cute little bottom in gear. We've got a big day ahead of us."

Rubbing the remains of sleep from her eyes, she blinked at him, and realized he was dressed. "Come back to bed, you fool. It's still early and—"

"It's past nine, and we need to get a move on," he interrupted, marveling at her beauty.

"Where to?" Roxana asked nervously.

He braced his hands on his knees and leaned toward her, kissing the tip of her nose. "We're going camping this weekend. I've already put the tent and the supplies in the car and—"

"Camping?" She drew back from him. "I'm not going camping," she assured him.

"Sure you are. It will be fun."

"I don't like to camp out. Why don't we stay here and spend the weekend in bed?"

"Because I don't want to be disturbed this weekend. If I hang around here, I'll get roped into spending time with the tournament guests. We'll find a nice, private place and pitch our tent. Then we'll drop a couple of lines in the water and catch our dinner. How does that sound?" he asked enthusiastically.

She pulled the sheet up to her chin and shook her head. "I told you that I don't like to camp out. It gives me the willies." She shuddered to emphasize her point. "You go on, and I'll stay here."

"Roxana..." His voice was filled with warning.

"No, Sonny." Roxana fixed him with a defiant glare. "I mean it! There's no way I'm going to traipse out into the woods where there are snakes—" she paused to swallow a lump of fear "—and sleep on the cold hard ground."

"Roxana..." he repeated, moving closer to her.

"No!" Her voice was fierce and her eyes hard with determination. "And that's my final word on the subject!"

Eight

Doesn't that look cozy?" Sonny asked, lifting the tent flap so that Roxana could see where their double sleeping bag had been carefully arranged.

"Cramped is the word that comes to my mind," Roxana said, refusing to give him any slack.

"Aw, Roxie!" He released the flap and grabbed his rod and reel. "Where's your sense of adventure?"

"Sleeping on the ground is an adventure I can live without." She glanced around the makeshift campsite where Sonny had pitched a tent and set up a folding table, on which he had placed a camp stove and an ice chest. "My idea of camping out is a fully equipped cabin or a luxury motor home."

"I'm going to catch us some fish. Do you want to help me?" he asked, hoping to win her over.

"I think you can manage that all by yourself," she replied, reluctant to fish when it wasn't absolutely necessary.

"Well, come with me and keep me company," he pleaded. Draping an arm around her shoulders, Sonny led her off toward the bank. "You can catch some sun while I catch some crappie."

After making their way through the tall grass and underbrush, they arrived at a pleasant spot on the bank. A flat rock jutted out over the lake, and Roxana draped herself over it, lying on her back and letting the sun stream through tree branches and toast her skin. Her navy-blue shorts exposed most of her legs, and she pushed up the sleeves of her powder-blue shirt and kicked off her tennis shoes.

"Better watch out." Sonny cautioned as he cast out his line. "Your skin looks like it could sunburn easily."

"What you really mean is that I'm as white as a ghost and will look like a lobster in an hour," Roxana corrected him, slipping on a pair of dark sunglasses.

His chuckle floated to her on a light breeze, and it warmed her in a way the sun could never do. From behind the protection of her glasses she admired him with unabashed devotion. His cotton T-shirt stretched across his broad shoulders, and muscles rippled across his back as he cast out his line again. The reddish-blond hair on his arms covered skin that had been tanned and toughened by nature's elements. Tufts of golden hair were visible in the V of his T-shirt, and Roxana remembered burying her face in that masculine forest the previous night and breathing the musky scent of him.

Her rapt gaze dipped down to his well-defined bottom and rock-hard thighs, hidden from her now by his faded jeans, but her mind recalled the intimate details, sending a shiver down her spine. A peculiar sensation erupted in the pit of her stomach, and she turned her face away from him. The telltale sign of desire made her blush and gently scold herself for her inability to look at him dispassionately. With a twinge of regret she recalled her holier-than-thou attitude toward Sheila Hawkins and her adoring article on Sonny. It would be difficult for her to write an article about him without undue prejudice in his favor. After last night she had lost any sense of journalistic objectivity where Sonny was concerned.

She closed her eyes and absorbed the peace and serenity around her. The gentle lapping of the water sang a soft lullaby to her, and the breeze caressed her brow as the world slipped away.

Sonny reeled in a flopping catfish and glanced at Roxana to boast, but the words died on his tongue. Was she asleep? he wondered, noticing the steady up and down movement of her breasts. He secured the fish on the stringer and plopped it back into the lake, tying the other end of the stringer around a hefty rock. He cast out his line again, then focused his attention on the woman who lay sleeping a few feet from him.

Damn if she wasn't the prettiest thing he'd ever laid eyes on! He'd never been with a woman who felt as good as she did in his arms. Her body was supple and mellow, without any of the hard edges he had endured with other women. She reminded him of the curvaceous pinup girls the servicemen had worshiped during World War II. The kind of girl you lusted for, dreamed of, and would have given a year's pay to be with for just a few stolen hours.

His fishing pole quivered in his hands, and Sonny tore his gaze from Roxana's prone body to the line that shimmered in the sunlight. His fingers wrapped around the corked handle. He gave a little jerk, hooked the tentative fish and reeled it in. The crappie's gray-and-white calico scales glistened as it fishtailed in midair, trying to escape the sharp hook. Sonny removed the hook and added the fish to the stringer. Then he cast his line to the same spot and settled down on a rock to wait for the next curious visitor.

Curious... He shot another glance at Roxana, and his brows met in a frown. As perfect as she seemed, something was amiss, he thought with growing suspicion. Sometimes she looked at him with those big, dark brown eyes and seemed to be begging for him to understand. But understand what? It was like working a jigsaw puzzle and not knowing what the overall picture was supposed to be. Other times he felt as if she were on the verge of telling him some deep dark secret, but she would clam up when he encouraged her.

Was there somebody else? he wondered. Was some other man waiting for her in New York? Had she just been feeding him a line when she had said that she wasn't seeing anybody special? There was nothing worse than shadowboxing a ghost, and he didn't want to be an unwilling sparring partner. He had told her about Sarah, so that Sarah's memory wouldn't come between them. Hadn't she extended him the same courtesy? Was she harboring someone else in her heart and dreaming about him right this very moment?

Roxana was dreaming about a man, a man who had turned her world topsy-turvy and made her evaluate what was important in her life. White lies rose like specters between her and Sonny, making the dream teeter on the edge of a nightmare. She fought them, punching air but doing little damage. They multiplied, keeping her away from the man who meant the world to her, and her flailing arms grew tired and limp until she could fight the apparitions no longer. Sonny began to dissolve in the hazy distance as the specters opened their hollow mouths and laughed with triumphant glee.

Roxana sat up with a strangled cry, emerging from the strange dream and finding herself in a shadowy world of water and earthy aromas. She reached up and removed her sunglasses. The shadows left with them, and she blinked against the welcoming sunlight. Her gaze flew to Sonny, and she smiled. He was still here! He was still hers.

"Are you okay?" he asked, holding out his hand and letting her clutch it with both of hers.

"Yes. I—I had a terrible dream. I dreamed that you left me," she explained.

"It was just a dream, honey. I've caught six fish since you dozed off," he reassured her.

"Really?" She released his hand and regained her composure. "That's terrific." Had he seen the desperation in her eyes? Did he know how pas-

sionately she loved him and how much she wanted
to keep him?

"Do you want to fillet the fish or start a camp
fire?" he asked, reeling in his line.

What a choice! She swallowed hard and wondered how she could refuse both job opportunities.

"Why don't you peel the potatoes and cut them
up? I'll fillet the fish and get the fire going," he
suggested when he received no answer.

"Okay." She slipped into her tennis shoes and
scrambled to her feet, accepting the easy chore before he could change his mind. She jumped down
from the flat rock and picked her way back to the
campsite, where she found the sack of potatoes and
a knife. By the time Sonny returned with the fil-
leted fish, she had peeled a dozen potatoes and was
slicing them into wedges.

"Are you hungry?" he asked, dropping the pail
of fish and moving to the heap of sticks he had
gathered earlier.

"Starved," she admitted.

"Good." He arranged the wood into a pyramid,
then struck a match and blew gently at it until the
dry sticks caught fire. "We'll fry those potatoes on
the camp stove. Do you know how to light it?" he
asked.

"I'm not sure." She examined the burner and
found lighting instructions printed on its lid. "Yes,
I can light it."

"Okay. Start up the potatoes, and I'll get these
fish to frying," he instructed, fanning the fire into
a pyramid of flames.

The simple task of preparing a meal with him
sent pleasure spiraling through Roxana, dispersing

her earlier objections to this camping trip. She set a skillet of grease on the burner, then dropped the sliced potatoes into the bubbling liquid while Sonny set a wire bracket over the fire and placed a deep pot on it, directly over the pyramid's apex. He sat back on his haunches, and his eyes found hers.

"I've got to wait until the fat gets really hot before I drop the fish into it," he explained, then tipped his head to one side in a gesture of wonder. "What are you smiling at?"

"I was just remembering some girl talk a couple of years ago," Roxana admitted. "Some of my women friends and I were discussing our ideas of the perfect man. They were naming characteristics like good sense of humor, tenderness, compassion, cute buns...." She paused to share in his burst of laughter. "And when my turn came, I told them that the perfect man would be a carpenter who could cook."

"What? No Greek god or knight in shining armor?" he asked playfully.

"I was being practical...or trying to be. I mean, a man like that could provide a roof over my head and food in my stomach."

"That's being practical, all right," Sonny agreed. "I must be darned near perfect in your eyes."

"You are," she whispered, and her heart lurched when her gaze met his through the curling smoke from the fire. He surprised her by blushing and averting his gaze. He hadn't blushed since the first time they had met under that strange veil of misunderstanding, and Roxana's heart melted. He could get to her so easily, she thought with a surge of tenderness that brought a mist to her eyes.

"So you're a woman of simple needs," he said after a few minutes of silence. "I bet that would surprise some people who think they know you."

"It surprises me sometimes," she said, happy to be totally honest with him for a change. "Before I came here, I thought I couldn't live without a microwave oven or mass transit." She laughed softly, shaking her head in bewilderment. "It's hard to believe that I'm without transportation and I haven't even missed it, or that I've existed on fish and hush puppies for days."

"But that's why you took up fishing, isn't it? To get away from all that stuff and live simply for a few days at a time?" he asked.

"I...uh...yes." She grabbed a spatula and flipped the potato slices. Why did he always have to throw her lies into her face?

"Have you ever thought of living simply all the time?"

"I have recently," she admitted, "but I don't know if I would enjoy it for a long period of time. I'm the kind of person who looks forward to a vacation, and then I'm ready to get back to writing after a couple of days." She sighed expansively. "I love to write, Sonny. It's not something I could give up easily. Writing is ingrained in me. It's part of me. I wouldn't be me without it."

"What has living simply got to do with your writing?"

She set the spatula aside and sought his blue eyes. "I thought you were suggesting that I resign and live here," she admitted.

He dropped pieces of fish into the bubbling pot of grease. "I was, but I didn't say anything about giving up your writing."

"My job is my writing," she explained.

"No, it's a form of writing. I wrote my first book at a campsite near Anchorage. I set up my portable typewriter and let her rip. I wrote my next book here at the resort, and my next one while I was jumping all over the country promoting my other books." He dropped the last piece into the pot and stood up. "Of course, if you think *Sportspeople* is the only thing you can write for, then you're rooted in New York, I guess."

Roxana found the conversation strangely disturbing. They were talking to each other, but there was so much they weren't saying. He was asking her to relocate here, but not necessarily with him, and she didn't know what to say or how to say it. She stared into the skillet of potatoes and frowned.

"I've fixed too much. We'll never eat all of these," she said, moving the potatoes around with the spatula.

"You're doing it again."

She looked up at his scowling expression. "Doing what?"

"Running away from things you don't want to face."

"And what am I supposed to be facing?" she asked with nervous curiosity.

"Us."

She shook her head. "You're pushing, Sonny. We've only known each other a few weeks and—"

"So what? After last night, are you telling me that there's no future for us?"

"I'm telling you that one night doesn't make a relationship!" Her voice rose along with her agitation.

"But it's the start of one," he stated firmly. "I'm pushing because you'll be leaving next week. We don't have a lot of time to examine what's happening between us."

She turned off the burner and set the skillet to one side. "The potatoes are ready."

He threw a pair of tongs onto the table. "Dip out the fish when they float to the top. I'm going to take a walk."

Roxana's eyes filled with angry tears, and she batted the tongs off the table in a burst of frustration. What did he want from her? Wasn't loving him enough for now?

Sonny propped his back against a tree and crossed his ankles in front of him. He regarded Roxana for long moments before he spoke.

"Are you going to tell me or keep it to yourself for a few more hours?" he asked, hoping she would finally confide in him.

Her dark eyes widened, and alarm shot through her. "Tell you what?" she mumbled innocently.

He laced his fingers on top of his stomach and sighed. "Ever since we got here, you've been on the verge of telling me something. Well, what is it?"

Roxana stood up and gathered their plates and eating utensils, stalling for time. Was she that transparent? she wondered. Had he known all along that she was nothing but a flimflammer?

She dumped the tin plates and utensils into the dishpan and looked at him. The truth welled within her, but fear stole the words before she could utter them. She wasn't worried about the stupid cover story anymore, she realized with a jolt. She was afraid of losing him. If she confessed, she knew he would turn away from her as he had from Sarah, and she couldn't stand to watch him leave her.

He shrugged, and disappointment twisted his lips into a frown. "Okay, forget it."

"No!" she cried. The need to make amends grew stronger until words spilled out. "I know Heather Rhodes."

His hands slipped to the ground, and he levered himself up to a straight-backed position. "You know her from where?"

"College." Roxana sighed with disgust at her own cowardice. Nothing like choosing the lesser of two evils. Tell him about the white lie, but keep that ugly black one to yourself. "She was my roommate for a few weeks."

"Have you talked to her since you've been here?" he asked with curiosity.

"Yes. She asked me to talk you into posing for the magazine, but I refused." She winced, realizing how easy telling that lie had been. "No, what I mean is that I agreed to talk to you about it if the subject came up, but I knew you would never agree to posing for their photographer."

"Why did you wait this long to tell me?"

"I—I don't know. When you asked me about her in Oklahoma, I wasn't sure it was the same Heather Rhodes. But when I saw her here, I realized it was."

"That's it?" he asked, his eyes narrowing with suspicion. "That's what you've been keeping to yourself?"

"Yes." She pressed her lips together tightly.

He pushed himself to his feet and strode to the tent. "Let's turn in."

"I'll wash these dishes first," Roxana said, moving toward the dirty stack.

"Leave them until morning."

"No, I want to do them now!" Her body stiffened until she heard him sigh and slide into the tent; then she slumped in utter defeat. She washed and dried the dishes by rote while her mind whirled in all directions. She had disappointed him. He didn't trust her. He had offered her an escape and she had run in the other direction. She told herself that when he discovered the depth of her deceit, he would never see her again...never hold her again...never love her again.

Her thoughts caused her to scurry into the tent. He was lying in the sleeping bag, his eyes closed, but the tense set of his jaw revealed that he was not asleep. Roxana stripped off her shoes, shorts and shirt and lay beside him. She kissed his stubbly chin, and his eyelashes fluttered.

"Good night, Roxana," he murmured.

She wrapped an arm around his waist, but he didn't respond to her embrace. Night sounds closed around her, and she shut her eyes and clung to him, knowing in her heart that she had lost him.

"So you've got the interview?" Bill asked with excitement in his voice.

Roxana sat on the hotel bed and cradled the phone to her ear. She felt cold, even though the midmorning sun spilled through the window and bathed her in a hot, buttery light. "Yes, I've got it," she replied with indifference.

"That's great!" Bill's voice welled with enthusiasm. "And you're still scheduled to compete in the tournament tomorrow?"

"Yes." Her voice sounded hollow to her ears.

"Fantastic!" Bill chuckled. "I knew you could do it! He doesn't suspect anything, does he?"

"I'm not sure," she admitted.

"Just bat those eyelashes at him, Roxie, and he'll stop thinking, period. He's a man and no different from any other—"

"Bill, this isn't a game! This isn't funny!" Anger coursed through her, chasing aside the cold emptiness within her. "I don't like lying to him. He's going to despise me when he finds out what I've done."

"He won't find out. Besides, you're there to get a story, not to win friends and influence people."

"This deceit goes against everything I believe in as a journalist. If you were a conscientious editor, you would have never asked me to—"

"Hold it right there, Miss Bendix!" Bill's voice shook with rage. "You're very close to getting fired from my staff! We're not stealing government secrets; we're just telling a hardheaded angler what he wants to hear, so ease up."

"We're *lying* to him. Don't try to pretty it up, Bill."

"What's with you, Roxie?" Bill asked. "If I didn't know better, I'd swear that you've fallen in love with Austin."

The silence was deafening, but Roxana could not utter a sound as the truth of Bill's statement rattled through her and made her heart ache.

"Roxie?" Bill's voice held a note of alarm. "Are you still there? Roxie, you're not really in love with him, are you? Roxana!"

She hung up, unable to answer Bill's questions. It was none of his business! She worked for him, but she didn't owe him an explanation of her innermost feelings.

Falling back on the bed, she let the phone ring until it died from lack of attention. Bill had to know by now that he hadn't been disconnected by mistake, and he was probably on the verge of firing her. So what? she thought. He had been wrong to make her come here wrapped in conspiracy, and she had been wrong to wear that tattered cloak.

She thought of last night when she had lain in Sonny's arms. Neither of them had slept, but neither had tried to scale the barriers they had erected, either. It had been the loneliest night of her life, and the loneliness had not lifted with the sunrise.

The light tapping at the door sent her hurrying across the room. She flung it open, hoping Sonny would be standing in front of her, holding out his arms to her. She groaned and turned her back on Heather.

"What's wrong?" Heather asked, stepping into the room and closing the door behind her.

"I thought you might be Sonny." A mirthless laugh tumbled from her. "Wishful thinking on my part." Roxana sat on the bed and stared at the celery-colored carpet. "I told him last night that I know you."

"Oh, I see." Heather sat beside her and placed a comforting arm around her slumped shoulders. "Was he livid?"

"No, I could have handled that. He was... remote." A sob tore from her throat, and she covered her face with her hands, ashamed of losing control in front of Heather.

"What's this?" Heather asked in a voice that reflected concern and confusion. She pried Roxana's hands from her face and stared into her watery eyes. "Did you tell him about your lack of fishing experience, too?"

"No, b-but I sh-should have," Roxana said between shuddering sobs. "I can't keep lying to him. It's tearing me apart."

"Then tell him!" Heather advised her.

"I'm afraid, Heather."

"Of what?"

"Of losing him."

"Oh, dear. I understand now." Heather stood up and crossed to the window. She shook her head in a sad, knowing way. "You've fallen in love with him, haven't you?"

Tears blurred Roxana's vision and tightened her throat until she could only nod.

"So fast? You've only known him a couple of weeks, haven't you?"

"It doesn't matter!" Roxana cried. "I love him. I couldn't love him any more if I had known him a decade."

"If you tell him that after you tell him about your little charade, he might forgive you."

"He won't." Roxana wiped her face against her sleeve. "He was in love with a woman who lied to him. When he found out, he sent her away and hasn't seen her since.''

''Oh, great,'' Heather said with a moan. ''What a mess! How did you land in this quicksand? You're the most honest person I've ever known. Why did you agree to this in the first place?''

''Ambition seduced me,'' Roxana admitted. ''I've been breaking my back at *Sportspeople*, and this chance at a cover came along and I just grabbed it without thinking or questioning my instructions. It seemed like a lark at first. A harmless little game that would get me what I wanted and push me up to where I wanted to be on the magazine.''

Heather kneeled in front of her. ''I know exactly what you're saying. I've been there. Ambition is a sword that can cut both ways, Roxie.'' Her green eyes explored Roxana's brown ones. ''Which is more important to you, Roxie? The magazine or Sonny?''

''Sonny,'' Roxana whispered.

''Then come clean with him,'' Heather advised.

''But there's a chance he'll never find out, and we can—''

''Begin a relationship with a secret between you?'' Heather asked, then shook her head. ''Is that what you want?''

''I want *him!*'' Roxana looked away from Heather, her gaze frantically bouncing around the room. ''If I'd only known how passionately I could love someone,'' Roxana murmured to herself. ''If I'd only known how much he would come to mean to me. If I'd only known!''

Nine

Jasper did a little jig to the song blasting from the radio, and Sonny grinned and clapped his hands in time with the beat. The older man's feet kicked and stomped the oval rug in the center of Sonny's living room, and he snapped his fingers and hollered with glee as he spun like a top, then did a fancy two-step at the end of the country-western classic. He fell into an easy chair and wiped his sweat-beaded forehead with his handkerchief.

"You can still cut a rug with the best of them," Sonny said, applauding long and loud for his friend. "Nobody can dance like you, Jasper. Nobody!"

Jasper chuckled and struggled for breath. "It's getting harder and harder for me to catch my wind after those little ditties. Whew!" He ran the handkerchief over his face again, then stuffed it into his shirt pocket. "But it sure feels good to let myself go every once in a while." He ran his hand through his thinning hair and nodded when Sonny offered him another can. "A beer would go down right fine, thanks. Say, what's wrong with you? Here it is the third day of the tournament, and you and Roxie are letting General Tee and Tim beat you! You've only got one more day of competition, you know."

"I know." Sonny handed Jasper a cold beer and took a drink of his own lemonade. "General Tee and Duncan are six ounces ahead of us, right?"

"That's right," Jasper agreed, running his sleeve over his mouth after he'd swallowed a large mouthful of beer. "Six ounces is a lot, Sonny boy."

Sonny sprawled on the couch, throwing one leg over the arm and letting it swing to the beat of the song on the radio. "Me and Roxie are having a bit of trouble."

Jasper's keen eyes narrowed. "Fishing or fighting?"

"We're not fighting. We're circling each other like two boxers waiting for the other to throw the first punch."

Jasper kept silent. He leaned forward, propping his elbows on the knees of his frayed jeans, and waited for Sonny to continue.

Sonny glanced at him and chuckled under his breath. "We've been polite to each other the past few days, but the tension is putting me through the wringer. Sometimes I want to grab her and give her a good shaking!" Anguish sliced through his voice.

"Why?" Jasper asked.

"Because she's…she's…" Sonny shook his head, unable to voice his real concern. "She's a puzzle, that's all."

Jasper fell back in the chair and stared thoughtfully at the beamed ceiling. "Ever get the idea that she's full of hot air?"

"What are you getting at?" Sonny asked angrily.

"I don't think she's fished all that much." Jasper glanced fleetingly at Sonny before his gaze returned to the ceiling. "She's not shooting straight."

Sonny lifted a shoulder in a careless shrug. "Most anglers are braggarts."

Jasper took a long drink and sighed. "You don't get the feeling that she's holding out on us?"

"Oh, hell!" Sonny sat up with a jolt. "Look at General Tee. You'd think he wrote the book on fishing, but he's won only a couple of tournaments. Everybody has their fish stories that are hard to believe."

"Right, but this is different. Don't get me wrong. I like the girl, but there's something funny about her. When it comes to fishing, she seems pretty green, so green that if you planted her, she'd grow."

Sonny chuckled at the analogy. "Well, you've got a point there. I can't remember ever meeting anyone quite like her."

Jasper's gaze bounced to Sonny. "You know, I'd hate to see you get your feelings trampled on again. You'd better keep your wits about you around her, Sonny boy, or you might get hooked by another woman like Sarah."

"She isn't like Sarah!" The flash of anger died quickly in him, and he smiled and laughed softly. "She's nothing like Sarah, Jasper."

"Well, if you say so," Jasper said, finishing the beer and crushing the can in one hand. "Think you can win this tournament?"

"Sure. Tomorrow will be better. See, here's my strategy. I'm giving General Tee and Duncan a sense of false hope, but tomorrow I'm going to pull that hope right out from under them."

"Strategy, huh?" Jasper asked with blatant disbelief. "Talk about somebody being full of hot air!" He poked a finger at Sonny and laughed. "Boy, it's a wonder you don't float right up to the ceiling!"

"You just wait, Jasper. You'll be eating those words tomorrow when they present me with the trophy."

"You and Roxie, you mean," he corrected Sonny.

"Yes, me and Roxie." He shook off a momentary veil of melancholy. "The tournament seems to be running like an oiled stopwatch."

"It is," Jasper agreed. "Biggest one we've had so far, and the best by all accounts. Everything is set for the banquet Friday night. We've got that bluegrass band all signed up to entertain us."

"Good. And you've got the trophies?"

"Sure do. They're all shined up and ready."

"Well, you might as well start engraving my name on the first-place one," Sonny said with self-assurance.

One corner of Jasper's mouth twitched. "I should have worn my hip boots tonight so that I could wade through all this bull."

Sonny grinned. "By the way, that reporter from *Pinup* lassoed me this afternoon."

"She did? What did she have on her mind?"

"Same old thing." Sonny finished the lemonade and set the glass on the table. "Now she's willing to settle for a picture of me clothed."

"That little gal is persistent."

"She sure is. She's an old friend of Roxie's."

"Come again?" Jasper levered himself up in the chair. "When did you find that out?"

"A few days ago. Roxie told me," Sonny confessed.

"Are they working together to get you to pose for the magazine?"

"No, it's nothing like that. It's just a coincidence." Sonny saw the glint of suspicion in Jasper's eyes. "Roxie doesn't care if I pose or not, which I'm not."

"Not even with your clothes on?"

"Oh, I don't know." Sonny stood up and paced to the empty fireplace. "I'm still thinking about that offer. I don't like that magazine, but Heather Rhodes seems like a nice enough woman. We had a drink in the club and a long talk. This assignment is real important to her and could mean a raise in pay."

"What will it do for you?" Jasper asked, his voice laden with concern for Sonny.

"Not much," Sonny admitted. "But I don't think it would really hurt me any. Tim Duncan is going to be their centerfold in that issue."

"You're pulling my leg!" Jasper charged.

"No, it's true." Sonny grinned at Jasper's flustered expression. "They've already taken the pictures of him. Heather said that he posed in a fishing boat; then they took some of him stretched out on the bank.''

"Holy Moses!" Jasper ran a hand across his face in a gesture of agitation. "I thought that guy had more sense."

Sonny chuckled. "So, you see? I'd be small potatoes. Nobody would even notice a picture of me with my clothes on. Heather promised to plug the resort. That would be worth it to me."

Jasper nodded, then grinned. "Wonder if they've approached General Tee. I'd like to see a picture of that old geezer in his altogether!" Jasper cackled and slapped his knee. "Wouldn't that be a hoot?"

A comical picture formed in Sonny's imagination, and he joined Jasper in a burst of laughter. "I don't think it would sell many magazines!"

"Hold on," Jasper said between chuckles. "I bet a bunch of old widow women would buy up copies. General Tee might become the sex symbol of the over-seventy group!"

The laughter died, and Jasper stood up and stretched.

"I gotta go," he announced. "Got to be at the dock by dawn. You'd better turn in, too, if you want to win this tournament."

Sonny placed a hand on Jasper's shoulder and walked him to the door. "See you bright and early, pal."

"Sonny..." Jasper opened the door, then turned back to face Sonny. "I know this isn't any of my business, but take care around that pretty little brunette. I love you like a son, and I don't want you to get into another mess like you did with Sarah."

Sonny cautioned himself to control his temper. He smiled and shook Jasper's hand. "Good night, Jasper. Thanks for the word of warning."

Jasper opened his mouth to speak, then pressed his thin lips together. He gave a short nod, turned and trotted down the steps and along the lighted walkway.

Sonny closed the door and leaned against it with a weary sigh. Jasper meant well, but it rankled Sonny when he suggested that Roxie was just like Sarah. With Sarah there had been no hope of redemption because she felt no remorse, no guilt. Lying was like breathing to Sarah; everybody did it, she had insisted, so what was the big deal? Roxie wasn't like that. If she was keeping something from him, she must have a good reason for it.

The past few days had been an ordeal of nervous tension that had begun that night in the tent when they had shared a double sleeping bag. Irony brought a sad smile to his lips when he remembered how he had looked forward to snuggling in that sleeping bag with Roxie and making love to her again. Ah, how the best-laid plans can go awry! he thought. That night had been one of the worst in his life. She had planted suspicion in his mind, and it had eroded his good intentions. Although he had wanted to hold her and kiss her, he could not bring himself to do it. He had lain awake, writhing in confusion and disappointment, not understanding his feelings or even why he had them.

He knew that until he could exorcise these feelings, he couldn't love her completely. It was hell to be with her each day and see the sadness in her eyes, to sense the mantle of agony she seemed to wear when she was with him. Maybe Jasper was right. Perhaps he should abandon his foolish hopes that everything would work out between him and Roxie. She didn't seem too anxious to relocate or find a way to be with him.

He jumped away from the door when the bell chimed. Had Jasper forgotten something? he wondered. He glanced around the living room, spotting nothing that belonged to his friend, then opened the door.

"Roxie!" He blinked, believing her to be an apparition. "I was just thinking about you."

"ESP," she said, peeking around him. "Are you alone?"

"Yes, come on in." He stepped back and let her enter, then closed the door. "Jasper just left."

"I know. I waited outside until he had gone." She placed her shoulder bag on the table by the door and turned to face him. Her eyes held that haunting sadness that twisted his heart. "I wanted to talk to you alone."

"I see." He nodded toward the living room. "Have a seat."

"Thanks." She sat in one of the easy chairs. "Could I have something to drink?"

"I have lemonade or—"

"Lemonade is fine."

He cast her an appraising glance before going into the kitchen for the drink. She was in a strange mood, he thought as he poured her a glass of the tart refreshment. Was she ready to confess? Ready to burn her bridges and start rebuilding? He returned to her, turned off the radio and handed her the glass.

"Fresh-squeezed," he said, smiling.

She tasted it and returned his smile.

He sat in the other chair across from her and noticed the tense set of her mouth and her stiff posture. "You seemed worried tonight. Does it have anything to do with the tournament?" he asked with concern.

"The tournament?" She visibly jerked, as if she had received an electric shock.

"Yes." Tension coiled within him until he thought he might break in half. "Jasper is worried that we might lose, but I told him we would come through with flying colors." When she continued to stare at him in silence, he tried a different angle. "Or is there something else on your mind?"

"I...I feel guilty," she admitted, tightening her hand around the glass.

Sonny breathed a sigh of relief. "Yes, go on. Talk to me."

"I'm afraid you'll hate me."

"Why would I hate you?" His fingers closed around the chair arms.

"Because...because..." She closed her eyes as a tremor coursed through her. "I'm afraid I'll lose the tournament for you and you'll never forgive me."

At first he thought he hadn't heard her correctly, but one look in her eyes told him that she was still dancing around the real issue. He leaned forward and ran both hands through his hair in utter frustration. "Oh, Roxie!"

"I've caught only one fish so far, and we're behind General Tee and Tim and—"

"Enough!" He shot up from the chair and balled his hands into fists at his sides. The urge to shake her until the secrets poured from her was strong, but he kept himself in check and glared down into her cloudy brown eyes.

"What's wrong?" she asked nervously.

"Everything," he said with a groan, turning his back on her and walking to the patio doors. He stared at the moon, racing across the dark sky and playing hide-and-seek with tufts of clouds. "If that's all you've got to say, then why don't you go back to the hotel? I'm tired, and I want to go to bed. I'm in no mood for this kind of discussion."

He stiffened when she caressed his shoulders and pressed her body against his back and hips. Shutting his eyes, he felt the stirring of desire and steeled himself against it.

"Roxana, please leave," he begged halfheartedly.

"Don't turn away from me, Sonny," she whispered, and he felt tears dampen his shoulder. "I need you tonight."

"No, go back to the hotel," he said, feeling his resolve weaken.

"I'm so lonely." She rubbed her cheek against his shoulder and moved her hands down his arms with a feather-light touch. "I ache all over because I know you don't want me anymore. Can't I stay here tonight?" she pleaded. "You don't have to touch me or kiss me or hold me. I just want to be near you."

"Oh, Roxie…" He sighed and opened his eyes to stare at the smiling moon. Did the woman in the moon know how defenseless he was against the woman who was stroking his arms in a restless, clinging way?

"I know I disappointed you by not telling you earlier about knowing Heather, but—"

"What's wrong between us has nothing to do with Heather," he interrupted, irritated that she continued to insult his intelligence.

"But you don't trust me, do you?"

He brushed her hands aside and turned to face her. "Before Sarah left, she told me that she loved me, and I couldn't believe her even though I wanted to. Is there any reason why I shouldn't trust you, Roxie?"

"I'm not Sarah," she stated flatly.

"I keep telling myself that, but it has a hollow ring to it these days."

She stumbled backward, and her lips trembled. "If that's the way you feel, then I should go." Whirling around, she went to the front door, but turned back to face him, her eyes brimming with unshed tears. "I've been thinking about doing that book on Reelfoot, but there's no point in it now that I'm an unwelcome guest." She picked up her shoulder bag and removed the diary from it. "I'll leave this with you."

"Wait a minute." He strode to her and gripped her shoulders. "Were you thinking of leaving the magazine to write that book?"

"Yes." She cast her gaze down, unable to look him in the eyes any longer.

"Roxie, Roxie," he murmured, pulling her to him and hating himself for it. "What am I going to do with you?"

"Make love to me," she whispered in a yearning voice.

"What will that accomplish?"

"It will make me feel better, and maybe it will make you feel a little better, too." She kissed the front of his shirt, then stood on tiptoe and pressed her mouth against his throat. "Be my friend, Sonny. I need a friend tonight."

"Why tonight?" he asked curiously.

Her breath was warm against his throat. "I have so much on my mind...so many things to sort out."

"Talk to me about it," he urged, struggling with the desire that was coursing through him.

"I can't yet." She wrapped her arms around his neck, and her eyes pleaded for understanding before her lips curved into a semblance of a smile. "Here I am throwing myself into your arms, and you want to talk."

He stared at her, finding no humor in the remark.

"That was a little joke," she said, trying to lighten the mood.

The aroma of her floral perfume swirled around him, and her body heat warmed his insides. Her eyes grew limpid, and he felt his reasoning twist out of shape like a piece of plastic held too close to a flame. What was wrong with loving her again? It might do some good for both of them. The closeness might bring down the walls between them and, God, he wanted that!

His arms encircled her waist, and his mouth flamed across hers. She gasped at his sudden change of heart, but responded to his savage kiss. Desperation and anger wove themselves around his desire for her, making him act with a wild, ferocious intensity. He began undressing her while raining bruising kisses on her face.

"Slow down," she whispered, her hands rubbing and stroking him. "Let me help."

He brushed her hands aside and removed her blouse and bra, her shorts and lacy panties. He carried her upstairs, placed her on the bed, then stripped off his own clothes.

Roxana held out a cautioning hand. "Don't love me in anger, Sonny. If that's all you're feeling now, then let me go back to the hotel."

Her words found their target, and he turned his head aside in shame. "Oh, Roxie, you've got me running in circles. I love you so much, I don't know what I'm doing. When I fall in love, I go deaf, dumb and blind."

"Fall in love?" she repeated, propping herself up on her elbows. "You love me?" she asked in a hesitant way.

"Yes," he whispered, feeling his anger subside, replaced with tender emotions. "Oh, yes."

Her smile was radiant, lighting her dark eyes and chasing aside the sadness that had been there for days. "Prove it."

His love for her spilled forth, and he gathered her into his arms and savored her lips. He tasted lemonade, tangy and sweet, and he flicked his tongue across her soft lips before probing inside. Her tongue moved against his, sending waves of trembling desire through him.

He loved her slowly and thoroughly, showering her with kisses from her lips to her toes. She murmured his name in a sweet, shuddering way and told him what she was feeling, how much she wanted him, and where to touch her. He brought her to the heights of passion, let her float back down, then lifted her to its peak again.

He moved deep within her, and she moaned with pleasure. He suckled her breasts, and she lavished him with praise. He pressed quick, hot kisses to her lips, and she begged for more. He released himself and quivered with the aftershocks, and she trembled with him and held him close until it was over.

And when it was over, he felt unfulfilled.

Sonny stared into the darkness while she slept in his arms and he felt cheated and vulnerable. Nothing had changed. They had communicated through their bodies, but they still couldn't talk to each other. Ever since they had met, they had talked around each other without getting to the heart of things. And tonight had not altered that sad condition.

Bittersweetness poured through him, bringing a mist to his eyes. He kissed the top of her head, knowing he had done all he could do. It was up to her now. She could take his heart and break it, and there wasn't a damned thing he could do about it.

Ten

_____

Reeling in his line, Sonny sat in a heap of desperation and began sorting through the lures in his tackle box.

"What time is it?" he asked Roxana.

She glanced at her watch. "Almost four."

He growled like an old wounded bear. "That leaves us with less than an hour, and we need another good-size crappie to have any shot at winning this tournament."

"We've got three keepers so far?"

"*Only* three, and *we* didn't catch them. I did," he said, picking up one lure after another and dropping them back into the compartments. "Where's my number-one, surefire, red-rooster crappie jig?" he mumbled with irritation.

Roxana glanced into the jumble of lures and pointed to a red one.

Sonny shot her an unnerving glare. "That's a bass lure, Roxie. Better batten down the hatches. Your incompetence is showing."

She lapsed back into the tense silence that had existed between them since dawn, when they had set out for their last day of tournament fishing, but her sixth sense shot a warning tingle down her spine. What was behind that cutting remark? she wondered. Did he know? Had she sold him short all this time by thinking that she had fooled him? She gave a mental shrug. It didn't matter anymore. As soon as this ordeal was over, she was going to confess to him and hope for forgiveness. She couldn't live with this lie between them. What had begun as an innocent deception had evolved into a cancer that was eating away at all her good qualities. She was an honest person and had always prided herself on that. No matter what, she had to regain her integrity.

Last night she had fully intended to tell him about her charade, but her own selfishness had won out. Looking into his eyes, she had realized that there was a chance she could spend one more night in his arms, and if she confessed to him, she knew she would lose that chance. In retrospect she wished she had gone through with her original plan, because last night had not been good for either of them. Physically it had been wonderful, but emotionally it had been barren. It had not brought them closer together but had pushed them farther apart.

Sonny mumbled vicious words under his breath while he continued to search for the elusive lure. Roxana glanced at him again and spotted the rooster jig pinned to his blue hat.

"It's on your hat," she said, reeling in her own line.

"It is?" He pulled off his hat and sighed. "So it is. Thanks." He plucked it off the brim and attached it to his line. "Let's try another spot. This one is the pits."

"Okay." She sat in the other chair and wished she could come through for him. She hadn't realized until the past few hours how desperately Sonny wanted to win this tournament.

He started the motor, and the boat whisked through submerged groves of cypress trees. Egrets rose from the branches, startled by the roaring motor. Roxana spotted a couple of water moccasins wound around one tree limb, but she gazed at them without the clawing fear she had known a few days ago. It was peculiar how quickly she had adapted to the sights and sounds of this earthquake lake.

Emerging from a narrow passageway, the boat shot toward an inlet that Sonny had identified earlier as Grassy Bend. He killed the motor, and the boat floated closer to the banks while Sonny used the trolling motor to position the boat in just the right spot. During the day they had tried several different spots, but none of them had been jumping with fish. Maybe this would be the one, Roxana thought optimistically, glancing at her watch and feeling the beginnings of panic stirring deep inside her.

Sonny cast out his surefire jig, and his face creased in concentration, as if he were sending mental messages to the fish. Roxana could almost hear his mind screaming, "Bite, damn you, bite!"

Roxana started to send her own lure out, but she stopped when she spotted the bucket of live bait. Minnows. She hadn't tried those yet because she loathed the idea of touching them. Would they be the magic that would change their luck? She remembered reading in her books that crappie liked minnows.

"I think I'll try a minnow," she said, pulling the bucket closer to her and staring down at the little gray bodies swimming inside it.

Sonny checked his electronic fish locater and tapped the screen with his forefinger. "There are fish around this boat, but you won't catch them with minnows. I've tried them, and the fish just aren't interested in live bait today."

Roxana dipped her hand into the bucket and grabbed water several times before she finally caught a minnow. It squirmed and slipped through her fingers. She tried again, caught one and held on. Repressing her squeamishness, she secured the slimy fish onto her hook, then cast it out near the bank. Wiping her hands on the legs of her jeans, she wrinkled her nose at the smell of wet fish, but sent up a prayer that something would bite.

"That's right," Sonny grumbled. "Don't listen to me. Why take my advice? You know everything there is to know about fishing."

"I never said that," Roxana disagreed, keeping a tight rein on her temper. Why was he baiting her today? she wondered. He hadn't said one kind word to her in hours. All he wanted to do was harp and complain and throw insults at her.

"Not in so many words, but you sure as hell implied it!" He glowered at her line. "And you won't catch anything that close to the bank, either! I told you that the fish were around the boat."

"Look, why don't you mind your own business?" she said, flashing him a murderous glare as her temper exploded. "I didn't ask for your advice, did I?"

"You can trust me," he charged, his blue eyes narrowing to slits. "We're partners, and I won't lead you down a blind alley."

A tingle of apprehension raced through her, and she looked away from him.

"If you've got something to say, just say it," she said, steeling herself for the inevitable.

"Instead of taking my advice, why don't you take your own?" he charged.

Roxana whipped around to face him, but he had turned his back to her and was staring moodily into the water. Her anger dissolved, and she wanted to reach out to him and erase his bad mood with loving kisses and caresses. Of course, it takes two to tango, she reminded herself, and Sonny was in no mood for dancing—or burying the hatchet.

"Here, fishee, fishee, fishee," he crooned over the side of the boat. "Dinnertime. Come and get it!"

She smothered a laugh and faced front again. There were so many things to love about the man. She adored his boyish quality, but she also appreciated his manly attributes. His sense of humor sent waves of giggles through her, and his more serious nature made her hang on his every word and deed. His many talents boggled her mind, and his simplistic life-style awed her.

Glancing over her shoulder, she watched as a breeze riffled through his hair. Oh, how she would love to run her fingers through his hair and kiss him until he trem—

Roxana straightened, and her fingers clutched her fishing rod. Another tremble ran down its length, and she cautioned herself not to jump the gun. Something was toying with her minnow, but it hadn't taken the bait yet. Wait...wait... wait...now!

She gave a little jerk, and her line grew taut. She had it! Suppressing the urge to squeal in joy, she reeled in the fish, taking care not to lose it. When she spotted the gray-and-white scales, she almost fainted from relief. Glancing at Sonny, she saw that he was oblivious to her activity. She grabbed the net, dipped it into the water and captured the hefty crappie. Only when she had lifted it from the water and removed the hook from its mouth did she lean over and tap Sonny's shoulder.

"What?" he grumbled, not turning around.

Roxana held the crappie by its lower lip and pushed it closer to Sonny's face. "Take a deep breath and smell success."

"What?" he repeated. "Where did you get that?" he shouted, whirling around and staring at the crappie.

"Over there in that spot where there aren't any fish," she said, unable to resist the gentle sarcasm. "And I caught it with a minnow."

A wry smile touched the corners of his mouth as he took the crappie from her and tested its weight before dumping it into the well with the other three.

"How much do you think it weighs?" Roxana asked, her voice brimming with excitement.

"Enough. It's about a three-pounder. I doubt if anyone else has caught one that big."

"Really?" Roxana dropped her rod and reel, realizing that it was over and that she wouldn't have to try her luck again.

"Really," he replied, reeling in his own line and setting the rod and reel aside before gripping Roxana's shoulders and delivering a hard kiss to her lips. "You came through for me, Roxie. I was hoping you would."

"So was I," Roxana whispered, still shaken by his kiss.

His lips touched hers again, lightly. His mouth moved against hers, lifting and pressing, sliding back and forth. Roxana closed her eyes, giving herself up to his expert ministrations. His tender kisses told her that there was still hope; things could work out between them if great care were taken.

He drew back from her, and his smile warmed her soul. "What time is it?"

She glanced at her watch and gasped. "We've got ten minutes to get back and weigh in!"

"We'll make it," he promised, setting her from him and starting the motor. "Hold on!"

Time nipped at their heels as they sped toward the resort. It seemed as if they were racing toward a confrontation that couldn't be avoided. After the tournament she had to lay out her transgressions for Sonny's inspection, no matter how hard that might be for her.

She had learned so many things about herself while she had been here in this hauntingly beautiful place. She had learned that a cover story for *Sportspeople* wasn't a particularly lofty professional goal, especially when she had to give up so much in return. Working in the confines of *Sportspeople* had twisted her ambitions and limited her.

In his honest, gentle way Sonny had opened her eyes and made her see the error of her ways. Would he believe her when she told him that she had never meant to hurt him and that she had hated lying to him? After his relationship with Sarah, it was doubtful.

The resort loomed ahead of them, and Sonny whipped the boat into a slip and secured it. He helped her leap from the boat, then grabbed their catch and raced ahead of Roxana to the weigh station.

"Here come Sonny Austin and Roxana Bendix!" Jasper said into a public address system. "There's less than a minute before the deadline. Will they make it, folks?"

Applause rose up from the spectators as Sonny bounded up the steps to the platform and handed over the four fish to be weighed. Roxana trotted up the stairs and stood beside him, her heart hammering away in her chest and her breath rasping in her throat. Her gaze darted between the scales and the lighted clock face that ticked off the seconds. Five...four—oh, hurry!—three...two...

"Nine pounds, four-and-a-half ounces," the man weighing the fish announced.

"Just in the nick of time," Jasper observed on the public address system, and a sigh of relief swept over the crowd. "Let's see here..." He checked his list of tournament fishermen and their totals, then lifted his gaze to Roxana and Sonny. "We've got a winner, folks. By the slim lead of half an ounce, the first place winners are Roxana Bendix and Sonny Austin! Runners-up are General T. Hayton Bainbridge and Tim Duncan. Congratulations!"

Roxana barely had time to absorb the announcement before Sonny tightly embraced her. He whirled her in a circle and rained kisses over her face. Roxana laughed, gripping his shoulders as the world spun around her. She closed her eyes slowly when Sonny's mouth came to rest on hers, and the world slipped away.

"I guess you're happy, aren't you?" he asked sarcastically when he finally withdrew his lips, ending the kiss.

"Happy?" she asked, feeling herself brimming with joy, but not sure they were talking about the same thing.

"Yes, you've got your story. That's what you came for, right?" His arms fell to his sides, and he turned and shook hands with Jasper, General Tee and Tim.

In a daze Roxana accepted their congratulations. Her mind whirled with confusion. She had won, but she had lost. She had gotten what she came for, but she was empty-handed. She had spent two weeks in heaven, but she was feeling like hell.

"The trophies will be officially presented tomorrow night at the banquet, so you all come," Jasper said, addressing everyone. "We'll have good food, good music and good times. It all starts at seven. Tonight there's a barbecue here on the front lawn at six, and you're all invited."

Roxana moved toward Sonny and placed a hand on his sleeve. "Sonny, I need to talk to you. Could I see you before the barbecue?"

"I...no," he said, tensing at her touch.

"No?" Her hand slipped off his arm, and she felt as if he'd slapped her.

"I've got a million things to do tonight, Roxie. I might not even make it to the barbecue. You know, the banquet and all..." He shrugged. "Sorry."

"I understand," she said, starting to turn away from him, but he caught her elbow.

"How about tomorrow before the banquet? About four o'clock?" he asked.

"All right." She nodded, feeling heavy with the weight of her guilt. She had hoped to lift the weight today, but now she would have to be burdened with it until tomorrow afternoon.

"Hello, Sonny. Hi, Roxana," Heather said, smiling at both of them as she approached. "Congratulations."

"Thanks." Sonny looked past her to the photographer. "I thought you guys would have packed up and cleared out by now."

"I hope you're in a good mood," Heather said, glancing back at the photographer, "because I'm going to ask you one more time to—"

"Save your breath, Heather," Sonny cut in.

"Just a picture of you with your trophy, Sonny," Heather begged. "Fully clothed, of course."

Sonny shook his head in a good-natured way. "I swear, you are the most persistent woman I've ever had the misfortune of meeting, Miss Rhodes."

"Please, Sonny? It's harmless, really."

Sonny glanced at Roxana and shrugged. "You've worn me down, Heather. Take your blasted picture."

"Oh, thank you!" Heather said, beaming with joy. "Step over there and pick up the trophy. This will only take a minute."

"Okay, okay." Sonny went over to the trophy and picked it up while the photographer issued instructions.

"Have you told him?" Heather asked, pulling Roxana to one side.

"I'm telling him tomorrow."

"Tomorrow, tomorrow, tomorrow," Heather chanted. "Why not get it over with now?"

"I'd like nothing better, but he's putting me off until tomorrow. He says he's got things to do tonight."

"Oh." Heather sighed and glanced in Sonny's direction. "Well, good luck, Roxie. I hope everything works out for you."

"Thanks."

"Look me up next time you're in California."

"I will." Roxana gave Heather a brief hug, then escaped the crowd of well-wishers. She didn't feel like celebrating. All she wanted to do was go to her room and have a good cry.

The following day Roxana returned from her sentimental journey around the resort and closed the door behind her with a wistful sigh. The long walk had been good for her, but had added to her sense of melancholy. A red light flashed on her phone. She had a message. From Sonny? she wondered.

She sat on the bed and dialed the operator.

"Yes, Miss Bendix," the operator said when she had asked for the message. "Bill Tidsdale called and said that you should call him when you have time."

"Thanks." Roxana replaced the receiver and fell back on the bed. She couldn't stand to talk to Bill now. He would be slap-happy about her winning the tournament, and she was in no mood for his cheerfulness. She might do something stupid like giving him a piece of her mind, and that would cost her her job. Her job was all she had left now.

Thoughts of returning to the magazine and New York saddened her. How could she be happy anywhere without Sonny? She would always be haunted by this place and the man who was rooted to it.

Sitting up, she glanced at the clock, then started getting ready for her meeting with Sonny. It would probably be her last visit to that charming A-frame house, and most likely it would be the last time she and Sonny exchanged civil words.

She changed into white slacks and a green lightweight sweater, brushed her hair, added a touch of blusher to her cheeks and set off on her mission.

Sonny was sitting in a metal chair on the front porch, his legs outstretched and his feet propped up on the railing. He gave a little nod as she mounted the steps and stood next to him.

"Afternoon," he drawled lazily. "Want some apple cider?"

"Yes, thanks."

"Help yourself," he said, pointing to the pitcher on a nearby table.

Roxana poured herself a glass. "Sonny, I—"

"How was the barbecue last night?" he interrupted.

"I don't know. I didn't go."

"Why not?"

She shrugged. "I was tired."

"Me too." He sighed, and a grin captured his lips. "We won! How about that? Boy, there were a few minutes there when I thought we weren't going to get our catch weighed in time, but we made it! Wouldn't that have been a heartache if we had missed the deadline?"

"Yes, a heartache. Sonny, speaking of heart—"

"The banquet is all set. It's going to be a real capper to a great two weeks," he cut in again, ignoring Roxana's look of desperation.

"Yes, but I—"

"Take a load off, Roxie," he said invitingly, patting the seat of the chair next to his.

"I'd love to take this load off," Roxana murmured, sitting and wishing he weren't in such a good mood. It made it all the more difficult to say what she had to say. "As a matter of fact, I came here to—"

"I was just thinking about the first time we met." He paused to laugh lightly. "What did you think of me then?"

"I thought you were special, and I still do."

He looked at her fully for the first time since she had arrived. "Oh, are we speaking truthfully now?"

Roxana expelled her breath. "Yes."

"Too bad. I was just getting used to playing the game."

"Sonny, I need to talk to you."

He set his glass of cider aside and stood up. "Come on in. If we're going to set things straight, we need to do it in private."

She nodded in agreement and followed him inside. Sonny stood in front of the fireplace and leaned back against the mantel. He motioned toward one of the chairs, but Roxana preferred to stand on her own two feet when she dropped the bomb.

"Sonny, I haven't been completely truthful with you." She took a deep breath, trying to ward off the tears that were building within her. "Remember Sheila Hawkins?" she asked. At his nod she continued, "Well, she did a horrible job with her article, and Bill Tidsdale, my editor, needed someone else to interview you again. Our fishing experts were on assignment, so he was left with me. I've covered court sports, like basketball and tennis, but never fishing. Bill showed me the letter you had sent that said how upset you were about being interviewed by someone who didn't know her subject, and he told me to pose as a seasoned angler to get the interview with you."

His jaw didn't drop. His eyes didn't widen. He just stood there, looking at her. Roxana swallowed hard and tried again.

"Sonny, I had never been fishing before except for one brief, unsuccessful expedition with my father when I was very young. I lied to you about everything."

"About everything?" he asked.

"Yes, well, about everything regarding my knowledge of fishing." She examined his taciturn expression, and the real truth hit her. "You knew, didn't you?"

"Yes," he admitted. "Your editor called me a few days ago and told me all about it."

"What?" She remembered the message from Bill and wanted to kick herself. If she had returned Bill's call, she wouldn't have walked blindly into this situation. "He told you everything?"

"He sure did. He apologized until he was blue in the face, and he said that you've been real upset from the beginning about lying to me."

"That's true," Roxana said, moving a step closer to him. "I wanted to tell you the truth. I really wanted to!"

"Why didn't you?"

"I had a case of tunnel vision." She threw out her hands in a helpless gesture. "I was wrong. I know that now, but all I could think about was my chance at the cover story, and everything else seemed insignificant. I know better now, Sonny." She took another step toward him, uneasy at his calm demeanor. Was it the calm before the storm, or couldn't he care less? she wondered. "I'm glad that Bill called you and apologized, but that doesn't let me off the hook. I'm a grown woman who makes her own decisions, and I decided to go along with his little scheme even though I had misgivings about it. It's been a valuable lesson and has set me back on the straight and narrow."

"How's that?" Sonny asked, crossing his arms against his chest and surveying her with outward aloofness, as if her confessions had not moved him or changed his mind about her.

"I've learned that people and their feelings are more important than a career." She could endure the intensity of his sky-blue eyes no longer, and she dropped her gaze and stared at her clasped hands. "I'm sorry, Sonny. My time with you has been golden, and I'll never forgive myself for tarnishing it with deceit." Tears rolled down her cheeks, and she turned and started for the door. The weight had not lifted as she had hoped it would. If anything, she felt more burdened now that she had confessed.

"It hasn't been all bad," Sonny said, and Roxana stopped and turned back to him. "I had a lot of fun watching you make a complete fool of yourself."

His cutting comment sliced through her self-pity. "What do you mean by that?" she asked suspiciously.

He pushed himself away from the mantel and walked slowly toward her. "Watching you put that minnow on the hook yesterday was about the funniest thing I've ever seen. It was all I could do to keep from laughing out loud."

She stared at him in stony silence, daring him to continue.

"And that day you fell in the lake and thought you were drowning," he added, laughing hysterically. "I wish I'd had a camera that day! I'd love to sell Heather Rhodes those pictures!" He smothered his raucous laughter, but his eyes were alight with humor. "If I hadn't been so in love with you, I would have seen through your pitifully inept act right off. Jasper knew you were full of hot air the minute he laid eyes on you."

Roxana squared her shoulders and glared at him. His teasing smarted, and she struggled to keep her temper at bay. "I'm glad I amused you, Sonny. If you ever need a good laugh, call me." She pivoted sharply and walked to the door, but Sonny closed the distance between them in a few strides and blocked her exit. "Now what? Haven't you gotten your pound of flesh yet?" she asked tearfully.

"While we're being truthful I just want you to answer one question for me."

She eyed him warily. "What is it?"

"Do you love me?"

It was the last question she had thought she would be asked to answer, and it stunned her into silence. Was this his final, cruel gesture? she wondered. Get her to say she loved him and then tell her that he didn't believe her? Roxana felt tears blur her vision and slip down her cheeks.

"Sonny, don't do this," she pleaded. "I'm sorry for everything. I know I've been a fool and that I've hurt you, especially after Sarah threw lies in your face. When you told me about her, it broke my heart, because I knew that I was no better than she. I'm hurting enough. Don't add to it." She held out her hand. "Can't we shake hands and be friends?"

"I don't want to be your friend," he said, grabbing her outstretched hand and jerking her to him so that she had to tip back her head to look into his eyes. "Answer my question!" he demanded.

A sob tore from her throat, and she buried her face against his shoulder. "Yes, yes! I love you with all my heart and soul!"

His hands smoothed down her hair, gentle and comforting. "Then where do you think you're going, sugar britches?"

"H-home." She sobbed again as the endearment registered. "I've done enough damage here. I'll go back to New York and mend my fences and try to forget you."

"Can't be done, Roxie," he whispered. His hands caressed her head and tilted it back so that he could look down into her tearstained face. "You'll never be able to forget me."

"I know." Her heart broke in two as the realization slammed into her. She would never forget him. And she didn't even want to. She wanted to remember everything about him, everything he had ever said to her, every moment in his arms...even this moment when it was all over.

"And I'll never forget you," he whispered, twisting Roxana's heart painfully. "I'm glad you came into my life and taught me how to love again, Roxie. I haven't been completely truthful with you, either." He smiled when she started to protest. "No, listen to me. I told you that I loved Sarah, but I didn't really love her. I realize that, now that I've met you. If I had loved Sarah as much as I love you, I wouldn't have been so quick to kick her out of my life. I would have tried to help her change her ways. But what did I do? I told her to hit the road, and I never really regretted it." A shudder coursed through him, and he gathered Roxana into his arms and held her so tightly that she could hardly breathe. "Good Lord, Roxana! I could never let you leave me like that. If you left, I would regret it for the rest of my life and spend all my time searching for you."

Although his admission filled her with joy, she tempered her elation. "But I'm just like Sarah and—"

"No, you're not," he said, his lips moving against her hair. "Sarah felt no remorse, but you're filled with it. You've been wanting to set things straight for days, haven't you?"

"Almost from the very beginning," she admitted, "but I was afraid of losing you. I kept chickening out because I couldn't stand the thought of living without you."

"So why did you tell me about it today?"

"Because I couldn't let the lie stand between us. I've never been a liar, Sonny. I've always been an honest person."

"I know. Heather told me."

"Heather?" Roxana leaned back and looked at him. "When did she get into the act?"

Sonny smiled. "You have staunch friends in your corner. Heather sought me out and spent a good hour telling me how wonderful you are—as if I didn't already know. She said she wanted to talk to me about posing with clothes on for her magazine, but that was just an excuse to sing your praises."

Roxana shook her head. "Heather Rhodes never ceases to amaze me. It was sweet of you to let her take those pictures. Maybe she'll get that raise she wants."

Sonny crooked a finger under her chin and lifted it. "I guess you'll get a raise once you write your article on me, right?"

"Yes, I might," she admitted.

"Too bad you have to resign."

"I do?" Roxana smiled, knowing where this conversation was headed.

"You have to write that book, remember?" he said, caressing her shoulders.

"Oh, yes. That's right."

His eyes narrowed to smoldering slits. "Besides, you have to come back here to me. And if you don't, I'll come and get you."

"Are you threatening to kidnap me?" Her hands moved up his arms and laced at the back of his neck.

"In the tradition of my ancestors," he said, nodding his head. "I'll kidnap you and keep you here until you fall in love with this place and with me."

"Oh, Sonny, now who's being foolish?" She pressed a light kiss to his lips. "Such drastic action won't be necessary, my love. I'm already yours, and I'd like nothing better than to put down roots in this lovely place."

His kiss dispelled her pessimism and filled the emptiness inside her. He gathered her up into his arms and took her upstairs to the bedroom where she had blossomed into a better person and a more complete woman. They undressed each other slowly, savoring the experience and telling each other the secrets of their hearts.

Their love united them, and they communicated not just with their bodies but with their souls. Spent passion brought tranquillity, and the specters of distrust lifted away. Roxana moved on top of Sonny and gazed long and lovingly into his clear blue eyes.

She arranged the silky hair on his forehead, and her love for him brought tears of joy to her eyes.

"I knew the first time I saw you that you were a dangerous man," she whispered between tiny kisses.

"Dangerous? I'm as harmless as a baby, honey."

"I know. What I meant was that I knew I had met my match."

"Oh, well, that's true," he agreed.

"Was I really that bad at fishing?"

He chuckled and kissed her soundly. "You won the tournament for us, didn't you?"

"Yes." She grinned, feeling proud of herself. "Yes, I did!"

"If you weren't a famous angler before, you are now. General Tee is already spreading the news that there's a new threat in the fishing world named Roxana Bendix."

"Oh, dear." Roxana sighed. "I wish he wouldn't do that."

"Why not?"

"Because now I'll have to live up to the legend."

"And defend your title at next year's tournament," Sonny said with a laugh.

"That's right!" Her eyes widened at the thought. "I'd better hire a tutor if I'm going to have a ghost of a chance at winning the tournament again next year. Do you know anyone who would give me lessons?"

He grinned, then fixed a thoughtful expression on his handsome face. "I've heard that Sonny Austin is a pretty good teacher."

"Yes, but I bet he's expensive. I probably can't afford him."

His hands moved down her back to cradle her hips, and she felt the stirring of his desire. "I imagine you could work out some kind of payment."

"You mean work it out in trade?" she asked, feigning innocence. "But what have I got that he would want?"

"Everything." The amusement left his face and was replaced by desire. "He's a greedy man, and when it comes to you, he wants everything you've got."

A trembling sigh escaped her, and she kissed him passionately. "I don't have any problems with that," she murmured. "Everything I have is his to take."

And he took what she offered and gave it back tenfold, continuing the long line of lovers who had found each other in this turbulent landscape and had carved out lives for themselves, against all odds.

Take 4 Silhouette Special Edition novels
FREE

and preview future books in your home for 15 days!

When you take advantage of this offer, you get 4 Silhouette Special Edition® novels FREE and without obligation. Then you'll also have the opportunity to preview 6 brand-new books —delivered right to your door for a FREE 15-day examination period—as soon as they are published.

When you decide to keep them, you pay just $1.95 each ($2.50 each in Canada) *with no shipping, handling, or other charges of any kind!*

Romance *is* alive, well and flourishing in the moving love stories of Silhouette Special Edition novels. They'll awaken your desires, enliven your senses, and leave you tingling all over with excitement...and the first 4 novels are yours to keep. You can cancel at any time.

As an added bonus, you'll also receive a FREE subscription to the Silhouette Books Newsletter as long as you remain a member. Each issue is filled with news on upcoming books, interviews with your favorite authors, even their favorite recipes.

To get your 4 FREE books, fill out and mail the coupon today!

Silhouette Special Edition®

Silhouette Books, 120 Brighton Rd., P.O. Box 5084, Clifton, NJ 07015-5084

 **Silhouette Desire**

COMING NEXT MONTH

CAUTIOUS LOVER—Stephanie James
Jess Winter was a cautious lover, but Elly Trent knew there was
warmth locked beneath his controlled facade. Perhaps playing the
seductress would provide the key. . . .

WHEN SNOW MEETS FIRE—Christine Flynn
Life in the frozen beauty of the Aleutian islands was exactly what
Dr. Tory Richards needed, until things started to heat up when
steel-eyed Nick Spencer literally crashed into her world.

HEAVEN ON EARTH—Sandra Kleinschmit
When Samantha met Jason she felt as if she had stepped into a
romance novel. But when she learned that he was actually her
favorite romance author, fact became stranger than fiction.

NO MAN'S KISSES—Nora Powers
Hilary had always tried to avoid Justin Porter, but now a debt forced
her to work on his ranch. Could she prevent herself from falling
under his spell again?

THE SHADOW BETWEEN—Diana Stuart
The sale of the McLeod mansion drew Alida Drury and Justin
McLeod together in the game of intrigue and romance that
strangely echoed the past and cast shadows on the future.

NOTHING VENTURED—Suzanne Simms
Wisconsin librarian Mary Beth Williams took a gamble and headed
for Las Vegas in search of excitement. She found it when she met
Nick Durand and hit the jackpot of romance.
